"I'm sorry I made you remember."

"Maybe it's just as well for me to remember. As long as the past festers in my heart, I'm not the kind of person God wants me to be. And the longer we work toward bringing Christmas to Yuletide, the more it makes me realize that I've not honored God by the way I've lived. My only concern has been Paul Spencer and no one else."

"I understand what you mean. Helping with the celebration and looking after the children has caused me to look at my own spiritual needs," said Carissa.

"We've been getting along pretty well the past three weeks, so let's forget our past problems and concentrate on finding Christmas—the way we'd planned. I believe we'll find it by caring for the children and bring Christmas to Yuletide."

Paul reached ut a hand to her, and with only slight hesitation, Carissa took it.

Books by Irene Brand

Love Inspired

IRENE BRAND

Writing has been a lifelong interest of this author, who says that she started her first novel when she was eleven years old and hasn't finished it yet. However, since 1984, she's published twenty-four contemporary and historical novels and three nonfiction titles. She started writing professionally in 1977, after she completed her master's degree in history at Marshall University. Irene taught in secondary public schools for twenty-three years, but retired in 1989 to devote herself to writing.

Consistent involvement in the activities of her local church has been a source of inspiration for Irene's work. Traveling with her husband, Rod, to all fifty states of the United States, and to thirty-two foreign countries has also inspired her writing. Irene is grateful to the many readers who have written to say that her inspiring stories and compelling portrayals of characters with strong faith have made a positive impression on their lives. You can write to her at P.O. Box 2770, Southside, WV 25187 or visit her Web site at www.irenebrand.com.

THE CHRISTMAS CHILDREN

IRENE BRAND

Published by Steeple Hill Books™

STEEPLE HILL BOOKS

Steeple
Hill™

ISBN 0-373-87244-5

THE CHRISTMAS CHILDREN

Copyright © 2003 by Irene Brand

Visit us at www.steeplehill.com

Printed in U.S.A.

For God so loved the world, that He gave His only begotten Son, that whosoever believeth in Him should not perish, but have everlasting life.

—John 3:16

To our friends, Rodney and Karen Dill,
who by example have given a new meaning
to the term "adoptive parents."

Chapter One

Darkness had fallen when Carissa Whitmore drove into Yuletide, New York, and parked her SUV in front of a fast-food restaurant. At first, she couldn't understand why she felt so let down, until she recalled her reason for being there. She'd come to this lakeside village to find the kind of holiday spirit she'd enjoyed as a child, but she couldn't see any indication of Christmas.

Carissa had anticipated a village ablaze with Christmas lights, nativity scenes and decorated trees, but except for the streetlights sparkling on the gentle snowfall as it filtered among the evergreen trees, the town was dark and uninviting. Stifling her disappointment, she entered the restaurant, sat at the counter to order a sandwich and a cup of tea. When she finished the meal, Carissa asked the waitress for directions to the police station.

The woman answered Carissa's question, then asked, "Are you the one who's moving into Naomi Townsend's house for the winter?"

Carissa smothered a laugh, but her blue eyes sparkled with mirth. She'd lived in a metropolitan area since leaving Minnesota twenty-five years ago. Carissa had forgotten how little privacy a person had in a small town.

"Yes, I am," she said. "I'm supposed to pick up the key from the chief of police."

The woman peered over the counter and nodded approvingly when she saw that Carissa wore boots. "I see you know how to dress for winter. It's only two blocks to the police station, but the streets are kinda slippery. It'll be safer if you leave your car parked here and walk, 'specially since you're from down South and maybe don't know how to drive on snow."

Carissa laughingly admitted that she had no experience with treacherous roads. When she lived in Minnesota, she couldn't afford a car.

She zipped up her heavy coat and stepped out into the chill air. The business section of Yuletide was located on the southern tip of Lake Mohawk—a small lake that measured four miles from north to south. Many vacation and permanent residences dotted the lakefront and extended into the wooded highlands.

Although Yuletide lacked Christmas ornamentation, it was a picturesque alpine village of small shops and businesses. Carissa looked forward to exploring the stores at her leisure, but she didn't dawdle tonight; the wind from the lake was penetrating her heavy parka. She gave herself a mental pat on the back for being wise enough to shop at a mall in Pennsylvania on her way north. Her Florida clothing wouldn't have been warm enough for Adirondack weather.

Warmth from a wood-burning stove welcomed Carissa when she entered the police station. The chief of police, a short sturdy man, sat behind a massive oak desk that dwarfed him.

"Hiya!" the chief greeted her. "I'm Justin Townsend. Mary, at the restaurant, called and said you'd arrived. We've been expecting you, but figured the snow had delayed you."

Carissa unzipped the front of her parka and shrugged out of the hood, revealing a head of short, curly blond hair.

"The highways were clear until a few miles south of Saratoga Springs. After that, I had to maneuver my way out of a dozen or more snowdrifts. I'd have stopped, but I didn't see any motels after the snow got so heavy."

Chief Townsend stood and reached across the desk to shake hands. "Welcome to Yuletide."

He took a ring of keys out of a desk drawer and handed them to Carissa. "Naomi's my sister-in-law. Sorry you missed her, but she left for Florida three days ago. She'd intended to show you around before she had to leave.''

''I was delayed at the last minute, and Naomi already had prepaid airline reservations, so I insisted that she go ahead. I called her on my cell phone this morning. She's already in Tampa enjoying the view of Tampa Bay from my eighth-floor condo. When I called, she was sitting on the balcony drinking a cup of coffee.''

A grin spread across the chief's broad face. ''Well, *you* won't be drinking coffee on *her* balcony in the morning.''

Justin gave Carissa directions to his sister-in-law's home. ''If you want to wait a while, I can drive out with you. My deputy will be back in a half hour.''

''Oh, you don't need to do that, unless the house is hard to find.''

''It's along the main road, but it's getting dark. I thought you might be a little skittish about going into a strange house and all.''

Carissa's even teeth gleamed in a wide smile. ''I've lived alone for more than twenty years, so I'm not afraid of an empty house.''

''No need to be,'' he assured her. ''Yuletide is noted for its low crime rate.'' He beamed expansively. ''I keep it that way. Remember, Naomi's house is the first two-story log house on your left, a mile north of town. There's a security light in the yard. We have someone in the station 'round the clock, so call if you need help finding the place. Drive carefully.''

Before Carissa reached the sidewalk, Chief Townsend stuck his head out the door. ''Naomi turned the temperature down. The house might be a little cool, but it'll warm up in a hurry when you raise the thermostat.''

Carissa waved her hand to indicate she'd heard him and hustled to her vehicle.

The drive along a narrow road, bordered by snow-covered evergreen trees, reminded Carissa of her childhood in Minnesota. And a wide smile spread across her face as she pulled up to the chalet she was to occupy for the next few months. The storybook setting was exactly what she'd been expecting.

Carissa had never met Naomi Townsend, but Betty Potter, a saleswoman for Cara's Fashions—Carissa's designing business—had called upon Naomi often. One weekend when Betty had been stranded in New York, Naomi had invited Betty to stay with her in this lakeside home. It was Betty who'd brought Naomi and Carissa together, when she'd learned that both of them wanted to spend the winter away from home.

The dusk-to-dawn pole light illuminated the two-story chalet with a soft glow. A porch, with waist-high banisters, hugged the house protectively, and a set of snow-covered steps led to the front door. Drifts blanketed the roof, and the evergreens in the yard bowed low under their accumulation of snow.

A sliver of moon hovered over the Townsend house, and Carissa remembered a portion of one of Whittier's poems: "The moon above the eastern wood shone at its full; the hill-range stood transfigured in the silver flood, its blown snows flashing cold and keen."

When she'd unwillingly memorized those words in an elementary school in Minnesota, Carissa hadn't suspected that she would ever find her way out of her dismal circumstances. But by sheer determination she had, and now stood in a setting that the poet could have been describing.

A cold wind discouraged Carissa from unpacking the car. She took the small bag containing her overnight essentials, walked up the steps and fitted the key in the lock. Expecting the house to be cold, Carissa was pleasantly surprised when a draft of warm air greeted her entrance. She could even smell food! Had she come to the wrong house? But the key had worked, so this had to be the Townsend home.

Carissa respected Betty's judgment, but still, she'd had some reservations about agreeing to occupy a home she hadn't seen. Her hesitation had been unfounded. The house could be a fitting subject for a magazine article.

She stood in the great room facing a fireplace encased in native stone. The room's furnishings were a combination of antique tables and chests with modern cozy chairs and upholstered couches. The vaulted ceiling was supported by rectangular logs, and a grandfather clock beside the stairway chimed the hour of nine o'clock as Carissa admired the setting. A teddy bear on the fireplace ledge gave the room a homey atmosphere.

Walking toward the kitchen, Carissa stopped suddenly. The television was on, although the sound was muted. Naomi had been gone for three days, and Carissa had understood that no one had been in the house since then. She looked at the thermostat, which was set at seventy degrees. Justin had distinctly said that Naomi had lowered the temperature. Had someone been in the house since then? Was someone there now? What other explanation could there be?

Suddenly, Carissa's lodging didn't seem so enticing. Should she telephone the police chief and ask him to check out the house? But if she'd misunderstood him about the thermostat, the man would think she was foolish. And she knew several people who never turned off their televisions. She reasoned that it had been a harrying day, and she was worn down, or she wouldn't be so skittish. Carissa's body ached for a hot bath and a comfortable bed, and she got ready to settle for the night.

She locked the front door and checked the windows, finding everything secure until she reached the sliding door that accessed a deck on the rear of the house. That lock had been jimmied. She turned on an outside light. The snow on the deck and steps was undisturbed, so apparently no one had entered the house through that door, but Carissa was uneasy knowing that someone *could* come in. Maybe people in Yuletide weren't as particular about locking their doors as she'd learned to be in a city.

Still, she knew she would rest easier if she had some kind of protection against unwanted guests. Barely over five feet tall, and weighing a little less than a hundred pounds, Carissa knew her appearance wouldn't intimidate a burglar. She didn't see a gun in the house, and she didn't know anything about firearms, anyway.

After years of experience in the business world, Carissa had learned to be resourceful. She brought several pans from the kitchen and stacked them in front of the door, moved two heavy chairs to provide a barrier, and put a set of fireplace implements in front of the chairs. Spying a decorative set of sleigh bells on the wall, she hung those across the entrance. It would be impossible for anyone to enter the room without waking her. But for added security, she took a poker from the hearth and carried it upstairs to use as a weapon if she should need it.

The master suite on the second floor had been prepared for Carissa—a large, comfortable bedroom with a connecting bathroom. A glass door, covered with heavy draperies, led to a balcony, and Carissa parted the curtains and peered through the door's frosty glass. Several inches of snow covered the balcony. Justin was right—she wouldn't be drinking her morning coffee outside.

Naomi had left a note on the pillow, and the words

"Welcome to my home" gave Carissa the feeling of a warm, gracious hug.

The room was cool and Carissa turned the switch on the electric blanket. While the bed warmed, she bathed. A few minutes later, bundled into a warm, ankle-length nightgown, Carissa laid the poker nearby and, sighing deeply, she stretched out in the warmth of the king-size bed. A Bible lay on the bedside table and Carissa reached for it. It had been a long time since she'd looked inside a Bible, but if she was going to be successful in her search for Christmas, she knew she'd have to start with God's word. She turned to Matthew's account of Jesus' birth and read a familiar passage aloud.

"'Now when Jesus was born in Bethlehem of Judæa in the days of Herod the king, behold, there came wise men from the east to Jerusalem, saying, "Where is He that is born King of the Jews? For we have seen His star in the East and are come to worship Him."'"

Carissa remembered enough from her childhood teachings to know that a person found Jesus through the eyes of faith. How strong was her faith? She believed that God had been her lodestar as she'd built a successful business. And she'd tried to repay Him by contributing a great deal of money to charitable organizations. To find the Christ Child, however, she'd have to go further than that. A Scripture verse she hadn't thought of for years flashed into her mind:

"You will seek me and find me when you seek me with all your heart."

Carissa had been hesitant about opening her heart to anyone, but she knew it was the only route to the peace found in the Savior who'd been born in Bethlehem years ago. She longed to experience the close fellowship she'd once known with God—the only thing that had sustained her through a difficult childhood. Would she find it in Yuletide?

The warm bed brought comfort to her tired body, and she thought she'd fall asleep immediately, but an hour later, she was still awake. She didn't consider herself an imaginative woman, but intermittent with the wind gusts that blew tree branches against the house, she thought she heard whisperings and muffled footsteps. Finally, she went to sleep—only to awaken suddenly.

Terror as strong as a bolt of electricity flooded her body as she struggled to a sitting position. She glanced at the illuminated dial of the clock on the bedside table. Three o'clock in the morning! What had awakened her?

Her pulse fluttered when she heard a muffled exclamation downstairs, a clatter of pans and the ringing of sleigh bells. Someone was in the house, and she knew it wasn't Santa Claus.

An intruder had stumbled over the barrier she'd placed in front of the glass door. Without waiting to put on a robe, Carissa jumped out of bed and grabbed the poker. Heart in her mouth and hands shaking, she was halfway down the stairs when the pale glow of the security light revealed a tall figure disentangling himself from her self-made booby trap. He groaned softly, and Carissa assumed he was injured.

She had left her cell phone in the car. If she went upstairs to use the phone on the bedside table, the man might follow her, and she'd be trapped. The man was between her and the kitchen phone. Her car keys were in the pocket of her coat, which she'd hung in the entryway closet. Realizing she was on her own, Carissa slipped down another few steps, just as the intruder stopped in front of her and looked upward. She swung the poker and hit him on the forehead. Carissa screamed as the man folded up like an accordion and fell backward on the floor. She'd only meant to stun him.

Jumping over his body, she sprinted to the kitchen and grabbed the wall phone. She dialed 911, and recognized Justin Townsend's voice when he answered.

"This is Carissa Whitmore at Naomi's home. A man just broke in. I'm afraid…I've killed him."

Dead silence greeted her remark for a few seconds, then Justin shouted, "Don't touch a thing! I'll be there in a few minutes."

Carrying the poker with her, Carissa rushed to her bedroom and tied a long robe over her nightgown. The intruder was stirring by the time she returned downstairs, and she breathed easier knowing he wasn't dead. Poker in hand, she waited by the door and kept a wary eye on the trespasser until a police cruiser screeched to a halt in front of the house.

Carissa opened the door, and Justin pushed by her into the living room.

He knelt beside the fallen man and checked his pulse before he took a quick glance around the room. When his gaze encountered the furniture in front of the glass door, he looked up at Carissa.

''What's happened here?''

''I sensed that someone had been in the house when I got here. I couldn't lock that door, so I piled things around it before I went upstairs to bed. This man came in, stumbled over my booby trap and awakened me. I hit him with a poker. Is he going to die?''

His eyes twinkling, the police officer said, ''Nope. It'd take more than a knock on his hard head to kill this man. Don't you know who he is?''

''How could I?''

''This is Paul Spencer, Naomi's brother.''

Carissa's breath rushed from her mouth, and she dropped like a deflated balloon into the closest chair she could find.

Chapter Two

$\backsim$

Still staring at the stranger spread-eagled on the floor, Carissa wrung her tiny hands and struggled to comprehend what Justin had said.

"I thought Naomi lived alone! Why would she exchange houses with me if her brother lives here?"

"Paul doesn't live with Naomi. He works for a construction company that bids on jobs all over the world. He hasn't been home for two years, and when he is here, he lives in the garage apartment behind the house. Naomi probably didn't know he was coming home."

Carissa stared at the tall, amazingly good-looking man, lying flat on his back. His dark skin had a weathered look, and his short brown hair, thinning a bit at the temples, had streaks of gray showing around his ears. A large blue knot had risen on his forehead.

"Oh, I'm so sorry!" Carissa said. "How can I face the man when he comes to?" Eager to justify her actions, she added, "But what would you have done if you'd thought he was a burglar?"

"Same thing you did, lady. Only I'd probably have shot him," he added with a grin, patting the holster at his right hip.

Chief Townsend called for an ambulance and said, "I'll keep him from moving until the medics get here. Don't look so scared. You had no way of knowing who he was."

When the prostrate man opened his eyes and started to sit up, Carissa dodged out of his range of vision. Townsend held him on the floor.

"Stay there, Paul. I don't want you to move until the ambulance gets here."

"What happened?" Paul said, a glassy expression in his dark eyes.

"I'll explain later. You'll be all right."

Paul closed his eyes again, and Carissa whispered, "I'll go upstairs and change. I'm going with you to the hospital."

"There's no hospital closer than Saratoga Springs, but we've got a clinic here in town. It's small, but it's a good one. The doctor there will be able to tell if he needs to go to the hospital."

The ambulance crew was working with Paul when Carissa finished dressing, and she waited until they pushed the stretcher toward the door. In her own car, she followed the ambulance into town until it stopped at a small building adjacent to the police station.

The waiting room had several people in it, and Carissa and Chief Townsend weren't able to sit side by side, which was a relief to her. She didn't feel like talking. Townsend seemed to know everyone in the room, and he told them in detail what had happened to Paul. Carissa tried to block out their amused chatter at her expense.

What if she had seriously injured the man? She knew better than to strike anyone on the forehead. Her only excuse was that she was half dazed after being awakened from a deep sleep. Carissa picked up a magazine and turned the pages slowly. She had no idea what she was seeing, for her thoughts were on the strange chain of events that had brought her to Yuletide.

For twenty years Carissa had worked relentlessly building Cara's Fashions—a line of casual clothing for tall women—into a prosperous business. She'd had no intention of selling, until the building where her corporate offices were located had to be razed for a road project. While she was searching for a new location, she was approached about selling her business.

She enjoyed her work, but the purchase price was high enough that Carissa seriously considered the sale. Considering led to selling, and within a few weeks, she was carefree for the first time in years.

When she was moving out of the office building,

she uncovered an antique trunk that had been sent to her after her grandmother's death fifteen years earlier. When she'd received the trunk, Carissa had put it in storage and forgotten about it, because she didn't like to be reminded of her past. But when she saw the trunk again, curious about its contents, she opened the trunk and found keepsakes from the past—textbooks, school papers and items she'd collected in Sunday school. She'd dropped those in the trash can, but she'd looked long at a large, white, wooden key decorated with golden glitter.

She remembered when, at six years of age, she'd carried that key in a Christmas pageant. She'd worn a long white dress, and appearing on stage, she had addressed the audience: "I have the key to Christmas, and I'm looking for a lock it will fit."

A first-century false-fronted village had been constructed on the stage with homes, a stable, an inn and several other businesses. She walked from door to door trying the key without luck, but when she found a lock that the key opened, a nativity scene was revealed. The Christ Child in the manger was Christmas personified, and Carissa had stood to one side while other church members presented the story of Jesus's birth.

To close the program, Carissa had turned to the audience, saying, "I've found Jesus, the reason we have Christmas. Won't you come to the manger and find Him, too?"

Carissa had known a close relationship with Jesus

as a child, and the observance of His birth had been a special time. Her grandmother couldn't afford to buy many gifts, and the church program had been the focal point of their Christmas. As the years passed, however, Christmas had gradually become commercialized for Carissa, a time when huge sales boosted her income, for Cara's Fashions were popular throughout the United States and overseas. Carissa hadn't been selfish with her income. In addition to contributing to many charities and churches, she'd provided freely for her grandmother until her death. Carissa had given generously of everything—except herself.

Her musings ended when the doctor entered the waiting room and asked for Chief Townsend. Carissa caught her breath, and cold sweat spread over her body. On trembling legs she moved down the hallway and peeped into a small room where Paul Spencer, eyes closed, lay on a hospital bed.

"He's all right," the doctor said, "and I don't see any sign of concussion, but he'll have a headache for a while. Exhaustion, more than anything else, caused him to faint." He turned to Carissa, saying with a grin, "You've got a pretty hefty swing, lady. You ever play baseball?"

Her face flushed, but Carissa tried to answer lightly. "Several years ago, I played on a women's softball team." She turned to Justin. "I'm so embarrassed about this that I've half a notion to leave without unpacking my car."

"Oh, Paul's a good sport and he won't blame you. He should have told someone he was coming."

"He could be released," the doctor said, "but he shouldn't go to sleep for a few hours. Paul hasn't slept since he left Europe, so somebody will have to keep him from dozing off. Since Naomi isn't home, he can stay in the clinic the rest of the night."

"He can come back to the chalet," Carissa said. "I'm responsible for his injury, so the least I can do is watch over him for a few hours."

"I'll go in and explain the situation. He might not want to trust himself to you," Justin said and guffawed. The doctor joined in the laughter, but Carissa failed to see any humor in the situation.

A few minutes later, she had to force herself to meet Paul Spencer's brown eyes when he walked into the hallway.

"Carissa Whitmore meet Paul Spencer," Chief Townsend said, humor still evident in his voice. "Although it seems you've met before."

"I'm so sorry, Mr. Spencer."

He shook his head and winced. "My fault! I should have let my sister know I was coming home. Our construction job had to shut down for a few weeks and I decided to come back to the States for Christmas. I tried to call Naomi when I landed at Kennedy. When she didn't answer, I came on home. The keys to my apartment are in her house, and I intended to knock on the door to get her attention. But when I discovered the door wasn't locked, I thought I could slip in without disturbing her and sleep on the couch until morning.''

''I'll drive you back to her house now,'' Carissa said. ''The doctor thinks you need monitoring for a few hours. Since I knocked you out, I'll feel better if I keep an eye on you.''

Paul agreed, and the chief of police accompanied them to the parking lot. An uncomfortable silence prevailed in the SUV as they drove through the business section of town. Carissa wasn't used to driving on snow-covered roads, so she drove as slowly and as carefully as she could. Her silent passenger gave her the fidgets.

''I'm so embarrassed I could scream,'' she said finally.

''I'm not embarrassed, but I am bewildered,'' Paul said, ''and it isn't all because of the crack on my head. I've got some questions. What prompted Naomi to leave her home and business and take off for Florida, and how do you come into the picture? When I talked to my sister six weeks ago, she didn't mention anything about leaving. Justin may have explained it to me, but my head was woozy, and I don't remember what he said.''

''We're almost to the house, and I'll explain when we get there, if that's okay. I'm not used to hazardous roads so I need to concentrate on driving.''

''I understand that. Take your time. I haven't driven on snowy highways for years. I drove cautiously from Kennedy, and that's the reason I was so late getting into Yuletide.''

When they entered the house, Carissa surveyed the disheveled living area with distaste. She'd replace the furniture and kitchen utensils later.

''Do you feel like a sandwich and maybe a cup of tea?'' she offered.

''That might be a good idea. It's been a long time since I've had any food, well, except for the pretzels and soda they served on the plane.''

''I'll see what I can find. I've only been here a few hours, and I haven't found my way around the kitchen yet.''

Paul followed her into the kitchen and leaned against a massive wooden post supporting the upstairs balcony that overlooked the living area. The kitchen was as inviting as the great room. Light oak cabinets blended with the pine-paneled ceiling. A food-preparation island filled the center of the kitchen. A round table was arranged in a window nook and four cushioned armchairs were placed around it. Several large, curtained windows blended in with the cabinets, to make the room light and airy in warm weather.

Carissa and Naomi had agreed that they'd put enough food in their refrigerators to last for a few days, but she saw now that the shelves were practically empty. That seemed strange, for in their business association, Carissa had found Naomi to be a woman of her word. There was a carton of orange juice and a gallon of milk in the refrigerator, both of which had been opened.

"We can have juice or milk. I don't see any sandwich fixin's, but what about a sweet roll? There are two left in the package. I can warm them in the microwave."

"I'll take coffee with the roll," Paul said, yawning and lounging wearily in one of the chairs at the table. "I haven't been to bed for about thirty hours. I may have to take a cold shower, too."

"It's cold enough outside to wake you up. Maybe you can take a run around the house."

"Not unless I have to," Paul said, shivering slightly. "It'll take a while for me to get used to Adirondack weather again."

Carissa heated water for coffee before she sat beside him. She said, "You already know my name, but I'll fill in some more facts. My home is in Tampa, where I've run a fashion design business for several years. I've never met your sister, but Townsend Textile Mill has manufactured many of my designs. Naomi and I have been in touch by phone and e-mail since she took over running the mill."

"That was when her husband died."

Carissa nodded. "I sold my business last month, and, being at loose ends, I decided I wanted to spend Christmas in the north. I was born in Minnesota, and I kept remembering the Christmases we had when I was a kid. By coincidence, Naomi's doctor suggested that she needed a vacation. He thought relaxation for a while in a warmer climate would ease the pain of her arthritis. A mutual friend arranged for us to exchange houses.''

''I'm happy that Naomi's taking some time off,'' Paul said. ''The pain has gotten steadily worse, and the stress of taking over management of the textile mill seemed to aggravate it.''

''That's what she said, We decided on short notice to make this exchange, and she probably didn't have time to let you know.''

''We don't stay in contact very well. Right now, my company's working on a project in an isolated part of Eastern Europe, and I call her when I get to a city. My cell phone doesn't work at our present location.''

Paul's eyes were glazed from lack of sleep, and when his head drooped, Carissa knew she had to keep him talking. ''What kind of work do you do?''

''I've been with the same construction company for eighteen years. I worked for them part-time in the States while I finished college, but since then I've been working overseas. Right now, we're building an electric power plant in the Czech Republic.''

''How often do you come home?''

''This is the fourth or fifth time I've been home since I left Yuletide about twenty years ago. I had an unpleasant experience here, and coming home reminds me of it, so I don't visit very often.''

He stifled a yawn. Carissa stirred a heaping tablespoon of coffee crystals into a mug of boiled water and handed it to him. He took several sips of the coffee before he continued.

"Last week, we had some equipment failure that will take a month to fix, so the boss told most of us to take a vacation. I usually spend my free time sightseeing in Europe and western Asia, but since it was Christmas, I had a hankering to be with family. Naomi is the only family I have. I'll have to go to Florida to see her, I reckon—I'll be returning to Europe sometime between Christmas and the new year."

"I have a two-bedroom condo, so there's plenty of room for you. I'm sure she'll be happy to see you."

"And I want to see her," Paul agreed. "I had looked forward to spending my vacation in snow country, but I've never been to Florida, so this sounds like a great opportunity."

"There's a good view of Tampa Bay from my balcony, and the beach isn't far away."

"You've convinced me," he said, laughing. "But I'll rest up a few days before I make any plans."

It was daylight by the time they finished eating, and Carissa exclaimed in delight as she viewed the frozen lake from the kitchen window.

"I was disappointed last night when I arrived in Yuletide," she said, "because it didn't have the Christmas atmosphere I had expected, but this area looks like the winters I used to know. There are lots of lakes in Minnesota, although we don't have mountains.''

While Paul showered and shaved, Carissa moved the furniture back into place and put the pots and pans she'd scattered on the floor in the dishwasher. She surveyed the room to be sure it looked as it had when she'd arrived. Something seemed to be missing, but she didn't know what until she realized that the stuffed bear she'd seen on the fireplace ledge wasn't there. She knew she hadn't moved it.

Paul returned at that time looking refreshed and more handsome than ever, in spite of his black eye and the bruise on his forehead.

''Did you move a teddy bear off the fireplace ledge?'' Carissa asked.

''No,'' he said, adding with a mischievous smile, ''I stopped playing with toys a long time ago.''

''Surely at forty-five, I'm not having a ''senior'' moment—as some of my friends say. But I know when I arrived last night there was a stuffed bear lying on the hearth. It isn't there now.''

''Maybe Justin or the medics moved it out of the way when they came for me.''

''Maybe. But I had the strangest feeling that someone had been in the house before I arrived. That's why I barricaded the door last night. The house was warm, although Justin told me that Naomi had lowered the thermostat before she left.''

''Maybe Naomi was having a senior moment, too, and forgot to lower the temperature.'' He looked out the back door. "I'm going over to check my apartment and put my rental truck in the garage."

Still brooding over possible intruders, Carissa walked to the wide glass door and stood beside Paul. Behind the house was a three-car garage with an apartment on the floor above it.

"We inherited this property from our parents," Paul explained. "When Naomi and her husband decided to build the chalet, I built the garage and apartment. I'm never in the States more than two months at a time, but when I'm here, I want my own place to stay in."

"It's a nice place."

"Good enough for what I need," he agreed. "Want to go with me and check it out?"

"Sure. I'm still your overseer for a few hours."

She grinned pertly at him, and Paul thought how fetching she looked. Carissa had intense blue eyes fringed by dark lashes, and a spray of freckles across her nose, which only added to the beauty of her delicate oval face. Carissa seemed young and untouched. Paul found it hard to believe that she was forty-five.

"I'll put on my boots and coat," Carissa said, wondering at the speculative gleam in her companion's eyes.

His apartment consisted of a large living room and kitchen combination with a spacious bathroom and bedroom in the rear. The absence of nonessential decorations proclaimed the apartment a man's. Carissa wondered at his age, judging that he was several years younger than she was. He'd said Naomi was his only family—but had trouble with a woman been the unpleasant experience that had caused him to leave Yuletide?

The apartment was chilly, and Carissa insisted that Paul go back to the house with her. "It'll be several hours before the apartment gets comfortable. By that time, you'll be ready to take a long nap."

"Thanks, I'll do that. But I wanted to point out the intercom system between my apartment and the house." He pointed to a speaker on the living room wall. "Just flip the switch and call if you need me. The one in the house is on the wall between the kitchen and the living room."

He yawned, and Carissa said, "Let's take a walk before we go back to the house. If you sit down, you're going to sleep."

"A good idea, but I'll need some warmer clothes, and I hardly remember what I have. I haven't been home during the winter for a long time." Paul shoved clothing back and forth in the bedroom closet until he found a heavy coat with a hood that still fit him. He changed his light boots for insulated ones.

Sunshine glistened on the newly-fallen snow as Paul and Carissa crossed the road and took the path around the lake. White-throated sparrows and Acadian chickadees darted into the trees, dislodging tufts of snow that settled on Paul's and Carissa's shoulders. They observed the ungainly flight of a pileated woodpecker, its red crest conspicuous in the sunlight. Small huts dotted the surface of the frozen lake, now covered with several inches of fresh snow.

"There's a lot of ice fishing on this lake," Paul commented. "The huts are rented to fishermen for protection from the wind while they wait for a bite."

"There's ice fishing on the lakes in Minnesota, too."

"I wonder if the lake is frozen enough for skating," he said. "I learned to skate on Lake Mohawk. We used to have skating parties almost every night. I've kept up with skating as much as possible. Many Christmas holidays I've spent time in Germany, Austria or Switzerland so I could skate." He stepped out on the surface of the lake. "Seems pretty solid. Do you skate?"

"Not since I was a child. Skating isn't a Florida pastime."

Their footsteps crunched rhythmically on the frozen snow as they walked. "Why did you leave Minnesota and move to Florida? Did your family transfer?" he asked.

A somber expression quickly erased Carissa's happy mood, but she answered readily enough. "I moved there by myself, soon after I graduated from high school. I never returned to Minnesota."

Believing he'd touched on a sensitive subject, Paul didn't question her further.

Carissa's animation returned moments later when she said, "This is the first time I've seen snow for years. It's glorious.'' She picked up a handful and ate it. ''Grandma used to make ice cream out of snow. I'll make some if I can remember how.''

''Most of my visits back home have been in the summer,'' he said, ''and I've missed New York's winters while I've been away. There were fabulous Christmas celebrations in Yuletide when we were children—lights all over the business section and most of the houses were decorated. Prizes were given for the most original ideas. We sometimes built snow palaces on the frozen lake and had them floodlighted. We had programs at the church—just a wonderful time.''

''Why did they stop? I came to Yuletide thinking I'd find Christmas the way it was when I was a child. I was really disappointed when I drove in last night and didn't see any sign of Christmas.''

Paul yawned. ''Carissa, surely I've stayed awake long enough. I'll tell you about the tragedy that took Christmas out of Yuletide, but not until after I sleep.''

Carissa was a bit surprised that they'd slipped so easily to a first-name basis, but that pleased her. Mischievously, she picked up a handful of snow and, standing on tiptoes, she rubbed it in his face.

''That oughta keep you awake 'til we get back to the house.''

''Hey!'' he spluttered, wiping the snow from his face with his mittened hand. ''I'm an invalid and you're supposed to be kind to me.'' He scooped up some snow and threw it at Carissa, but she side-stepped the attack and started toward the house on a run. Paul's long-legged stride soon caught up with her.

"I'll get even with you," he warned, a gleam in his brown eyes that belied his words. "I expected to be welcomed home as an honored guest, and what happens? I'm assaulted the minute I step into the house, and then I get my face washed with snow."

Laughing, Carissa said, "I'll make it up to you. While you take a nap, I'll fix a meal for you."

"Sounds good to me, just as long as I find a bed before I fall asleep on my feet."

While Paul slept in the downstairs bedroom adjacent to the great room, as silently as she could, Carissa unloaded the SUV and carried her luggage upstairs. Periodically, she'd crack open the bedroom door, and each time, Paul's even breathing assured her that he was resting comfortably.

She would have to wake Paul before too long because the doctor wanted to look him over again. She organized her belongings in the master bedroom, then sat on a padded window seat looking over the frozen landscape. Her thoughts were on Paul Spencer.

He seemed like a friendly, easygoing guy, possessing a spontaneous cheerfulness that answered a need in Carissa's heart. She'd never considered herself a joyful person, but when Paul's mouth spread into a toothy smile that lightened the darkness of his face, Carissa felt lighthearted, and laughter bubbled from her lips.

Having a man in the house was a strange experience for Carissa. She'd never known who her father was, and her grandmother had been widowed before Carissa was born. She'd lived alone for more than twenty years, and it seemed odd to have a man sleeping in her house. She had grown accustomed to solitude, but already she knew she'd miss Paul a little when he moved into his apartment.

Carissa had come to Yuletide to discover the faith she'd known as a child, and she was determined to achieve that goal. It had taken a long time, but Carissa finally believed that she could do whatever she set out to do.

Yet she'd never reacted to anyone as she was reacting to Paul Spencer. Her attraction to him confused her.

She found his nearness disturbing and at the same time exciting.

Chapter Three

Carissa retrieved the Christmas pageant key from her luggage and carried it downstairs. She placed it on the coffee table. Confronted by Paul's presence, she needed a constant reminder of why she was in Yuletide.

Paul was still sleeping at one o'clock, so Carissa tapped on the bedroom door. He didn't respond, so she knocked more loudly.

"Uh-uh," he said sleepily. "What is it?"

"You have to see the doctor at three o'clock. It's time to get up."

Silence greeted her. Had he gone back to sleep? She knocked once more.

"I'm sorry," Paul said. "It's taken me a few minutes to realize where I am. You're the lady who's taken over sis's home, huh?"

''Yes, the one who attacked you with a poker last night.''

''Do you have the poker now?''

She imagined his white teeth showing in a slight smile. With laughter in her voice, she said, ''Not yet, but I may have to get it if you don't hurry.''

He yawned noisily, and she heard his feet land on the floor.

''Be out in a minute.''

Carissa was standing at the back door appreciating the landscape, when the bedroom door opened behind her.

She turned, stifled a gasp and experienced a giddy sensation as if her heart had flipped over. Paul had the broad-shouldered body of an athlete, but his waist and hips were narrow. Wearing a T-shirt and jeans, he leaned against the door, looking as vulnerable as a child. His eyes were still heavy with sleep and his hair was tousled. He yawned again.

Had she been wrong when she'd made up her mind that she could live a happy, fulfilled life without a husband? Was she old enough now that the pitfalls she'd avoided in her youth would no longer tempt her? Was it possible to disprove the opinions of her childhood neighbors, who'd often said ''Like mother, like daughter''?

Deep in her own thoughts and conflicting emotions, Carissa started when Paul said, ''It won't take me long to get ready. I'll bring in some fresh clothes from the car.''

She winced when she noticed that the bruise had spread until both eyes and part of his cheek were black.

Intercepting her glance, he said, "I could pass for a raccoon this morning, don't you think?"

Blood rushed to her cheeks, and she covered her face with her hands. "Don't remind me. Does your head hurt?"

He lifted his hand to his forehead. "No, but it's sure sore to the touch. I don't dare turn my head quickly."

Dropping her hands, Carissa said, "I'll get your luggage."

He started to shake his head, thought better of it and said, "Thanks, but I need a jolt of Adirondack air to help me wake up."

"I made some lunch so we can eat before we go. There isn't much food in the refrigerator, but I'll stop at a grocery store after we've been to the clinic."

"I'll need to buy a few groceries, too, though, I'll probably eat out most of the time. When I'm home for such a short time, I don't want to store up any food."

Carissa was tempted to suggest that they could share their meals, but she hesitated. At her age, this was no time to become involved with a man. After all, she didn't know anything about Paul Spencer. She wouldn't become chummy with this stranger.

Why, then, did her heart insist that Paul wasn't a stranger?

*   *   *

Carissa sat in the waiting room, and when Paul came from the doctor's office with a smile on his face, she felt a great wave of relief.

"There's no damage except a sore head for a few days. I can live with that," he said.

"I don't know that I can," Carissa said. "I'll probably have nightmares for years about you collapsing at my feet. I thought I'd killed you."

"I'm glad you didn't," he said. He laid his hand on her shoulder.

Carissa flinched and moved away, and his hand dropped limply to his side. Paul stared at her, slightly embarrassed, a confused expression on his face. He must be wondering why she would be offended at such an innocent gesture.

Carissa knew that Paul only meant to be friendly, but she wasn't used to casual touching. She'd denied any natural tendencies toward overtures of friendship for so long that she had a complex about being touched. Several years into her career, she'd finally conquered her phobia enough to shake hands with her customers, but she apparently hadn't overcome all of her hang-ups.

Being friendly and outgoing had contributed to her mother's undoing. She could do nothing about looking like her mother, but long ago Carissa had determined that she wouldn't emulate her mother's personality and lifestyle. Her mother's vivacious personality had gotten her involved with the wrong people and sent her down the path to prostitution and, ultimately, premature death.

Embarrassed that she'd allowed a phobia from the past to make her reject Paul's overture of friendship, Carissa lifted a flushed face to him. Her blue eyes mirrored her anxiety. Her voice was strained when she said, ''I'm glad, too, that I didn't injure you,'' and she added in her thoughts, *for several reasons.*

Paul wondered at the anxiety revealed in Carissa's eyes. She was a successful businesswoman...but had he detected a flaw underneath the facade that she presented to the world? At this moment, she seemed like a bewildered little girl unable to understand what had happened to her. For several years, Paul had made it a point to tend to his own business and keep aloof from the problems of others. Now, for some inexplicable reason, he longed to remove that confused, lonely expression from her face. Before the next few weeks passed, he would no doubt learn if it was in his power to do so.

As Paul moved his belongings into the apartment, he kept thinking of Carissa. When Jennifer had jilted him, he'd made up his mind he was through with women. He'd deliberately chosen a job that would keep him out of the United States. He hadn't been tempted to seek the companionship of women in the countries where he'd worked, and, most of the time, he was content with his bachelorhood.

Occasionally, Paul wondered if he was missing

anything by not having a family. If he didn't have any children, who would carry on the Spencer name and family traditions? He often questioned what would become of the money he'd accumulated, if anything happened to him—for his sister didn't have any children, either. And what could Naomi do with the fortune she'd inherited from her husband? It was only in the past year, since his fortieth birthday, that Paul had become concerned about this issue.

Carissa was an attractive woman, and he smiled when he thought of her embarrassment over hitting him on the head. But, personally, he thought it took a lot of courage to attack a man with no better weapon than a poker. Paul admired courage in anyone.

She was a little woman—her head didn't even reach his shoulders—but at times she displayed a dignity that belied her short stature. And Paul had detected a lot of warmth and vitality waiting for release beneath that dignity.

He sensed that Carissa didn't think she was beautiful, but beauty was in the eye of the beholder. After the way Jennifer, who was tall and shapely with black hair and vivid green eyes, had treated him, Paul had decided that he'd never choose another companion based on outward appearance.

From what he'd seen of Carissa, he believed her beauty was more than skin deep.

Paul saw his sister so rarely that he was disappointed to learn that Naomi had gone to Florida.

He'd called from Kennedy Airport to have his home phone connected, so he asked Carissa for the telephone number of her condo so he could call his sister. He tried three times before he finally found her at home. She couldn't believe he was actually in New York.

"Why didn't you tell me you were coming home?" Naomi cried in dismay. "I would have stayed in New York. But you can come here," she added. "The weather is wonderful. I go to the beach every day for several hours, and I'm feeling better already. I've even decreased my pain medicine."

"I'm glad to hear that, sis. I'll come down for a few days before I go back to my job." The logical thing for him to do was to go to Tampa immediately, but as strange as it might seem to him, he wanted to see more of Carissa.

"I'd come home," Naomi continued, "but I can't because I've loaned the house to Carissa for two months. Have you met her?"

"Well, yes, we had an...unusual meeting."

He explained how they'd met, and Naomi laughed merrily before she said, "I can't imagine what happened to the door. I'm sure it was locked when I left home. Will you have it fixed?"

"Yes, I intend to."

"How do you like Carissa?"

"She's okay," Paul said nonchalantly. Naomi's ultimate goal was to see her brother married and settled down in the United States. He didn't want his sister to read anything into his meeting with Carissa. "She was embarrassed at first about hitting me, but we laugh about it now."

"Carissa is a very successful businesswoman. She sold her company for a bundle a few months ago. I've been told that the sale netted over a million dollars. And you should see this luxurious apartment!"

Paul thought he'd accumulated quite a lot of money, but he certainly wasn't in Carissa's league. His attraction to Carissa had reached its first barrier. He wouldn't fix his interest on a woman who was worth more financially than he was. But in spite of his reservations, after he'd finished his dinner, Paul kept searching for an excuse to see Carissa again that evening.

As she often did at home, Carissa prepared a taco salad, sat in front of the television and watched the evening news while she ate. Before she'd sold her company, her days had been so busy with business matters that she didn't have much of a social life. It was usually a relief to escape into her apartment at night and let the walls close around her. Her only relaxation was at the health club in the basement of the condo complex. She'd made some good friends there, and she missed them tonight.

She'd gotten a sack of Red Delicious apples at the grocery store, and while she munched on one for dessert, she reflected on her day with Paul. This time yesterday she'd never heard of the man, but they'd gotten acquainted in a hurry. Had the time come for her to seek the male companionship she'd previously avoided? Now that she'd reached the mellow years, the hang-ups she'd had about dating shouldn't be a problem. It was rather astonishing that she was even thinking about the subject, and most surprising was that she hadn't had such thoughts until she met Paul Spencer.

"Hey, neighbor!"

The loud voice startled Carissa so much that she dropped the apple core on the floor. It took a moment for her to realize that Paul was calling on the intercom.

"Hey, neighbor!" The call came again before she remembered where the speaker was.

Smiling, she picked up the apple core, hurried into the kitchen and answered Paul.

"Hey, yourself."

"I wanted to see if this thing still works. What are you doing?"

"Finishing dinner."

"I promised to tell you why Yuletide is no longer a Christmas town. If you have time, I'll come over and fill you in."

"Great! I'd like some company."

Humming a Christmas song that she'd just heard on the television, Carissa rinsed the dishes she'd used for supper and put them in the dishwasher. She prepared a bowl of grapes, cheese cubes and crackers and placed the food on a table between two large lounge chairs in the living room. She poured a jar of fruit punch over ice and was placing it on the table when Paul knocked on the back door. She motioned him inside.

"Brr!" he said, taking off his coat and laying it on the back of the couch. "The temperature is dropping quickly. If it wasn't already, the lake should be frozen enough that I can go ice fishing tomorrow. If I make a nice catch, I'll invite you to have dinner with me in my apartment."

"Can you cook?" Carissa asked as she motioned him to one of the chairs. It seemed rather odd to be acting as hostess to Paul in his sister's house.

"I'm a fair cook," he said. "I've prepared dinners many times for some of my co-workers. But I'm not such a good fisherman, though, so don't whet your appetite for a fish fry until you see the fish."

"Help yourself to the snacks," Carissa invited.
"I'll take you up on the invitation. I'm *not* a good cook— I just make what satisfies my appetite, and that's not always what others like to eat. I never cook a meal for anyone. If I have guests, I take them to a restaurant for dinner."

"Since I kept you up most of last night, I hesitated to barge in on you—you'd probably like to go to bed early. I'm sleepy, too, but I want to adjust to Eastern Standard Time, so I'm forcing myself to stay up."

"Good idea. I haven't done much overseas travel,

but it usually takes a week for me to get over jet lag.''

Paul poured a glass of fruit juice and sipped it as he talked. ''As I told you earlier, when I was a kid, Yuletide was just like a fairyland during the Christmas season. But a tragedy one Christmas Eve changed all of that.''

He paused, stretched out his long legs and continued. ''That night, a woman and her baby came to town asking for shelter. She went to several businesses and private homes, as well as the police station, but everybody was too busy to help. The people didn't mean to be callous, but they just expected the next person to take care of her. No one did, and on Christmas morning the woman and child were found dead, huddled in the entrance to Bethel Church.''

''Oh, how terrible!'' Carissa said feelingly, and memories of her own neglected childhood surfaced.

''The woman had fled from an abusive husband, and she died from complications of an unattended childbirth. The temperature went to zero that night and the baby died from exposure.''

What a tragedy! Carissa could understand the reason the citizens of Yuletide hesitated to celebrate Christmas.

''The strange part of it was that the church was presenting a program that night based on an old legend of how Jesus had appeared disguised in a town one Christmas Eve. Disguised as a child, a poor woman and a beggar, He went from person to person asking for help, but everyone was busy preparing to celebrate the coming of the Christ Child, and they turned these people away.''

''I'm familiar with the story. The townspeople eventually learned that if they'd helped those who came to them, they would have received Jesus, too. So the citizens of Yuletide felt that in refusing to help the mother and child, it was as if they'd refused, like those people or the biblical innkeeper, to shelter the baby Jesus?''

Paul nodded and lifted a hand to rub his forehead. Although he hid his discomfort well, obviously he was in pain.

''No one could generate any enthusiasm for a big celebration after that. Although I consider it superstition, the general feeling seems to be that when God has forgiven the people of Yuletide for neglecting those two people, He'll give them an opportunity to redeem themselves.''

''Wouldn't it be wonderful if this is the year?'' Carissa said. ''I came to Yuletide looking for the Christmas spirit I had as a child.''

''What made you start looking at this time?''

''I sold my clothing design business a few months ago, and when I was cleaning out the office and storage room, I found a trunk that my grandmother had left to me. My uncle had shipped it to me after her death. There wasn't anything valuable in it—mostly memorabilia that I'd kept since my school years. I trashed most of the things, but I kept this—''

She picked up the white key, and Paul thought Carissa had forgotten his presence as her mind took her quickly down memory lane.

''When I was about six, I participated in a program at our church, and I carried this Key to Christmas. I went from place to place trying to fit the key into a lock, and when I finally found a door the key would open, a nativity scene was revealed. When I came across this key a month ago, I realized how far I'd strayed from the teachings I'd learned as a child. I knew then that I had to find a wintery place to relive the Christmases of my childhood. I didn't want to return to Minnesota because it doesn't hold pleasant memories for me. Besides, all of my close relatives have died. It seemed like a coincidence that Naomi wanted to change locations at the same time I did.''

''As far as that's concerned, I need to be reminded of what Christmas really means, too. Carissa, I hope you *can* revive the meaning of Christmas that you once knew. Maybe we can find it together.''

Their eyes met and held for a minute before Carissa looked away, too confused to even answer. She swirled the liquid in her glass, thinking that she was acting like a child.

''I guess it's time for me to go,'' Paul said. ''I'm getting sleepy now. And you must be tired, too, unless you slept while I was napping earlier.''

She shook her head. ''No, I didn't sleep. I unloaded the car and settled in. Thanks for coming over tonight.''

She held out her hand to him, and, unsuccessfully stifling his amazement, he tenderly clasped her hand in his.

Without meeting his gaze, she said, "Your gesture in the doctor's office took me by surprise, or I wouldn't have reacted so foolishly."

"It was just a friendly gesture," he assured her.

"I know. A foolish quirk of mine caused my reaction. I'll tell you about it someday. And I hope we can become friends." With a warm grin, she added, "It's always a good idea to make friends with your next-door neighbor."

Carissa fell asleep easily, not even worrying about the unlocked back door; she felt protected with Paul nearby. But she woke up suddenly, about the same time she'd awakened when Paul had entered the house the night before.

She'd heard something. Carissa sat up in bed to listen. The sound seemed to come from the kitchen, and she eased out of bed, wishing she'd kept the poker upstairs. Vowing that she would secure the back door before another night, Carissa ran quickly and silently downstairs.

When she reached the last step, she said, "Who's there?"

She heard a gasp and a scurry of feet.

Too frightened to be careful, Carissa snapped on the lights and rushed into the kitchen, just in time to see the pantry door close. She pushed a table in front of that door.

Standing beside the intercom, she shouted, "Paul! Paul! I need help."

Although it seemed like hours, it probably wasn't more than a minute before she heard Paul's muffled tone. Poor man! She thought, somewhat humorously, that she'd ruined another night's rest for him.

"What's wrong?"

"Somebody is in the house. Come help me."

"I'll come right away. Be careful!"

She took a knife from a cabinet drawer for protection if the intruder should break out of the pantry.

Paul rushed in the door, dressed only in pajamas and slippers, rumpled hair hanging over his agitated brown eyes.

"In the pantry," Carissa stammered.

Without asking questions, Paul motioned. "Get behind me."

He pushed the table away and swung open the door, his body hunched forward, ready to attack if necessary.

"Come out!" Paul commanded.

Nothing could be heard for moments except Paul's heavy breathing. Then there was a scuffling of feet, and Carissa stared, slack-jawed, disbelief in her eyes. Beyond words, she lowered the knife.

A teenage boy sauntered out of the pantry, followed by a little girl who held one of the red apples that Carissa had stored in the pantry. Another girl, probably eight or ten years old, peered around them, holding in her arms the teddy bear that Carissa had seen beside the fireplace the night she'd arrived.

The knife slipped from Carissa's hand and clattered to the floor. She pulled out a chair from the table and slowly lowered herself into it to support her shaking legs.

"Any more where you came from?" Paul asked, peering into the pantry.

The boy shook his head. The smallest girl handed the apple to Paul; the other child started crying.

Carissa's body trembled and a wave of nausea seized her. She dropped her head into her hands. She'd come to Yuletide looking for solitude so that she could experience a renewal of mind and spirit. She hadn't had a minute of peace since she arrived. Within twenty-four hours, four people had invaded her house.

What had given her the foolish idea to look for Christmas in Yuletide?

Chapter Four

The children bore a marked resemblance to each other, so they were obviously siblings. Of slight stature and build, the children had light brown hair and dark brown eyes. The oldest girl wore glasses, and the boy had a blue cap on his head. The smallest child sidled close to the teenage boy, and he put his arm around her.

Speechless, Carissa stared at the three children.

Paul recovered his composure more quickly than she did, and he asked, "What are you kids doing here?"

The smallest child looked at Paul fearlessly, but the boy dropped his head.

"Tell me," Paul insisted. "Who are you and what are you doing here?"

Carissa noticed that the children were shaking, and she doubted it was all from fear.

The older girl's sobs sounded as loud as thunder, and they reached a soft spot in Carissa's heart. "Just a minute, Paul," she said.

The children seemed malnourished, and the sorrow in their eyes was unmistakable. Their clothes were worn out, and not very clean. She moved to the sobbing girl and knelt beside her.

"Are you hungry?"

Without looking up, the girl nodded. Paul and Carissa exchanged looks of compassion. Suddenly, Carissa realized why there had been so little food in the refrigerator when she arrived. These kids had broken into the house and had been living off the food Naomi had left. Carissa's arrival had probably kept them from getting any food for the past two days.

She knew that the sensible thing to do was to call the police, but Carissa suddenly remembered her own impoverished childhood. She couldn't turn these children away until she learned what circumstances had brought them here.

"Then you sit at the table, and we'll fix something for you to eat. Paul, if you'll warm milk for hot chocolate, I'll make sandwiches."

The children scuttled toward the table.

"That's my chair, Lauren," the smallest child said, and preempted the chair the older girl had started to take.

Paul and Carissa exchanged amused glances. As he opened the refrigerator door, Paul said in an undertone, "Apparently, they've eaten here before."

"Seems like it," Carissa agreed. She lifted a package of lunch meat, mayonnaise and a loaf of bread from one of the shelves. "What are we going to do with them?" she whispered.

Paul shrugged his broad shoulders. "Feed 'em."

While the milk heated, Paul set out three mugs. Carissa made several sandwiches, cut them into quarters, and arranged them on a plate that she set before the children.

"Go ahead and eat," she said. "The hot chocolate will be ready in a minute."

She looked for a package of cookies she'd bought earlier in the day. If the children hadn't eaten much, she didn't want them to founder, so she put six cookies on a tray and took the package back to the pantry.

Paul noticed the moisture that glistened in Carissa's eyes while she watched the hungry children gobble their food. The children were still shaking, and Paul, thinking it might be from cold as well as hunger, said, "I'll raise the temperature on the furnace."

Carissa turned to put the sandwich fixings back in the refrigerator. As she worked with her back toward the children, she prayed silently. *God, here's a problem I don't know to handle. Who are these children? What should I do with them?*

Remembering the legend she and Paul had discussed a few hours earlier, she continued talking to God. *Is this situation like the one that confronted the people of Yuletide several years ago? Has your Son come tonight personified in these children? Should I treat them the same way I'd treat Jesus if He came to my house?*

Recalling her early biblical training, Carissa thought of the verse ''I was hungry and you gave me something to eat...whatever you did for one of the least of these...you did for me.''

Was this a spiritual test? She'd come to Yuletide to find Christmas. Would she relive the birth of Jesus through these children?

Aware that Paul was motioning her toward the living room, Carissa went to him, and he said quietly, ''What do you want to do?''

''There may be a search going on for these kids. We should call the police, but...'' Carissa hesitated. ''I think I'd rather hear their story first.''

''That's my gut feeling, too. They've apparently been living in this house for several days. Another hour won't hurt anything.''

Paul had started the coffeemaker earlier, and when he and Carissa went back into the kitchen, he replenished the chocolate in the children's cups and poured a cup of coffee for Carissa and himself. Paul pulled out the other chair for Carissa at the table, and brought another chair from the living room. He sat where he could face the children.

Watching Paul warily, the boy nibbled on a cookie.

''All right,'' Paul said sternly. ''Let's have it. Who

are you? What are you doing here? And why shouldn't we turn you over to the police?''

The smallest girl started to speak, and the boy put his hand over her mouth.

''I'll do the talking,'' he said.

''My name's Alex. These are my sisters, Lauren and Julie. Lauren's eight, Julie's six.''

''And your age?'' Carissa asked.

''Fourteen.''

''That's all right for a start,'' Paul said. ''What's your last name?''

Alex shook his head.

''Does that mean you don't have a last name or you won't tell me?''

''I *can't* tell you.''

''Where's your home?''

The boy shook his head again, a stubborn set to his features.

Paul laid his hand on Alex's shoulder. ''It's obvious you kids are in trouble. You'd better tell me what's going on. If possible, I'll help you, but if you've run away from home, your parents must be notified.''

''We ain't got no parents,'' Julie said.

''No home, either,'' her sister said, and started crying again.

Turning on his sisters, Alex said angrily, ''I told you I'd do the talking.''

''You're doing fine, girls. Go ahead and talk,'' Carissa said.

"Our mommy died," Julie said, and she slipped out of her chair and crawled up on Paul's lap.

With a helpless look at Carissa, he put his arm around the girl when she cuddled against him.

"You've got a half hour, Alex, before I call the police," Paul said.

"I ain't tellin' you our name or where we lived. Nobody wants to find us, anyway."

He looked belligerently at Paul, who stared at him until Alex dropped his head. After a slight hesitation, the boy continued. "Our mother has been real sick for two years. Something was wrong with her heart. We took care of her the best we could, and the neighbors helped, too. But she died, anyway, about two months ago."

"Where's your father?" Carissa asked.

Alex shook his head.

"Is he living?" she persisted.

"We don't know. He left when Julie was just a baby. We ain't seen him since. I don't think he's dead, though. Every so often, we'd get some money that we figgered he'd sent. No word from him since Mom got sick, so he might be dead, for all we know."

Paul's arm tightened around Julie, and he looked at Carissa, whose face was white and drawn. Lauren was still crying, her head on the table. Carissa moved closer and put her hand on the girl's trembling shoulder. She looked as if she was ready to start crying, too.

The misfortune of these children had reminded Carissa of how bereft she had been when her own mother died. If her grandmother hadn't taken her in, where would she be today?

"Surely you have some other relatives who will take care of you until your father can be found," she said around the knot in her throat.

"Just aunts and uncles. None of them wanted to take three kids, so they planned that we'd all go to separate homes in different states," Alex said. "We'd never have been together again. Mom wouldn't have wanted that. Nobody could agree on who was gonna take us, so we stayed in our home until the rent was due. The preacher and his wife kinda looked after us."

Lauren lifted her head. "We didn't want to be parted. So we run away."

Julie had relaxed in his arms, and Paul realized that she'd gone to sleep. "We'd better have the whole story before we decide what to do with you," he said. "Alex, you can't go on like this."

"We've been traveling from place to place on buses for two weeks, sleeping in bus stations, but when we got to Yuletide, we didn't have much money left. I was in the grocery store in Yuletide and heard your sister say she was leaving for Florida for two months. I found out where she lived, and thought we could stay here for a little while. I didn't know anyone was going to be living here."

"Obviously you've been eating food from the

kitchen, but where have you been staying?'' Carissa asked. ''Last night I was sure there was someone in the house, but where have you been in the daytime?''

''In the furnace room. We took some blankets from the bedroom and fixed our beds. It was warm down there, and nobody could see the lights at night. We stayed on this floor during the daytime.''

''I can't understand why you thought you could get away with this,'' Paul said. ''Where'd you get the money to ride on buses?''

''Our neighbors collected some money for us to use until we could find a home.''

''This is incredible!'' Carissa said. ''I'd think there would be a nationwide hunt for you.''

''Maybe nobody knows we're gone,'' Alex said, a crafty gleam in his brown eyes.

''What does that mean?'' Paul said severely.

''Alex wrote notes to our aunts and uncles so each would think we were with another one. He left a note for the preacher that we'd gone to visit with our uncle in—'' Lauren broke off the sentence when Alex shook his head at her.

''Alex, what kind of kid are you, anyway? You lied to your family, you jimmied the lock and came into my sister's house, and you've been stealing food from her kitchen. I know you're young, but can't you comprehend how much trouble that's going to cause you?''

Alex straightened in his chair, an indignant expression in his brown eyes. He pulled a piece of paper from his pocket. "I didn't steal nuthin'. I kept track of all the food we took," he said, adding, "so I can pay it back someday."

He handed the paper to Paul, whose throat constricted when he read the daily entries: "three glasses of milk, three sweet rolls, three sandwiches."

Paul passed the paper to Carissa.

"I was only trying to look after my sisters. What would you have done if it had been you?" Alex asked Paul directly.

"I don't know," Paul admitted, looking toward Carissa.

"Shall we all go back to bed and decide what to do in the morning?" Paul asked. "Aren't there twin beds upstairs?"

"Yes."

"Then let's put the girls in that room." He paused thoughtfully. "My brother-in-law had a game room in the basement. I'll check that out to see if Alex can sleep there. But first I'll carry Julie upstairs. She's already asleep."

Cradling the child in his arms, Paul headed toward the stairs. "I'll be back in a minute," he said to Carissa.

When Paul came downstairs, he said, "Alex, let's get you fixed up for the night."

Taking Lauren's hand, Carissa climbed the stairs. Julie was lying on the bed, so Carissa didn't bother with nightclothes, even if the children had any. She removed the girls' shoes and covered them with a warm blanket in the twin beds that were ready. Impulsively, Carissa leaned over and kissed both girls on the forehead before she went downstairs.

Carissa paced the floor and waited for Paul. The few hours she'd spent in the house had been so hectic that Carissa didn't even know that there was a basement. When Paul returned, he entered the room from a door to the left of the fireplace that she'd assumed led to a closet.

"Well, what did you do with him?"

"I found just the place for him," Paul said. "After my brother-in-law died, Naomi closed up his game room, saying she couldn't go to the room alone. I knew where the key was, so I put Alex there. In addition to a pool table, there's a sleeper sofa. Alex tumbled into bed as soon as I spread out some sheets. I think he was asleep before I left the room. It smells a little musty, but it's warm. Now what do we need to do?"

They eyed each other for a few moments until Carissa said, "Pinch me, so I'll know if I'm dreaming. Is this really happening?"

Paul moved closer and pinched her gently on the arm, and she didn't mind his touch at all.

"Unfortunately, you're awake. And we have a problem on our hands."

"You're telling me! Three problems, actually. Should we telephone the chief of police now?"

"Probably we should, because we could be legally liable for not reporting the kids." Paul glanced at the mantel clock. "But it's four o'clock in the morning. I don't think it will hurt to wait 'til daylight. Justin probably couldn't do anything tonight."

"I feel so sorry for them. I hate to turn them over to the police—but what else can we do?"

"Let's decide later." Uncertainty crept into his expression. "Even if they're only children, we don't know what danger they pose, so I don't want to leave you alone. It wouldn't surprise me if Alex tries to sneak out of the house tonight and take the girls with him. That's the reason I separated them. Will it be all right if I sleep in Naomi's room tonight? I'll leave the door open so I can hear Alex if he tries to leave. Poor kid. He's probably been taking care of his sisters for months."

"Please do stay here. I doubt I'll sleep, anyway, but I know I won't if I'm here alone with our self-invited guests."

Carissa's feet seemed as heavy as lead as she went to her room. So much had happened in the two nights she'd spent in Yuletide that her former life as a businesswoman in Florida might never have happened. When she'd taken the road to Yuletide, she'd felt like a woman on a mission—a pilgrim taking a nostalgic journey into the past. But she couldn't reconcile her reason for coming north with all the things that had happened. Thirty-six hours ago she had never heard of Paul Spencer or these children, yet in a short time they'd affected her life so much that she wondered to what extent they would have an impact on her future.

Carissa hadn't expected to sleep, and she didn't. Her thoughts were filled with things that she'd successfully pushed from her consciousness years ago. In her mind's eye, she was back in Minnesota, the weather similar to what she'd experienced today. She sat in a bleak upstairs bedroom, wrapped in a blanket, hovering over her mother's dying body. Only six years old at the time, she didn't know that her mother was a prostitute dying from a drug overdose. She only knew that she was losing the person she loved most in the world. She'd felt forsaken, unwanted, unloved.

Carissa knew her mother was dead when her grandmother came into the room and pulled the blanket over her daughter's emaciated, rigid features. Carissa could almost hear her own whimpering as Grandmother Whitmore gathered her into her loving arms.

"Come, child," Grandmother had said patiently. "There's nothing we can do for her anymore. It's all in the past. Let's see what we can do with your future."

Where would she have been today if it hadn't been for her grandmother's love and tenderness during the next twelve years?

Apparently, there wasn't a grandmother to look after her present household guests. Who would see to their future?

Chapter Five

Carissa hadn't realized she'd gone to sleep until she was wakened by a small hand tapping on her shoulder.

"Hey! I gotta go to the bathroom."

Startled, Carissa's eyes flew open. Momentarily, she couldn't comprehend where she was, or why this child was in her Florida condo.

Shaking her head to clear it and smothering a yawn, she finally said, "Good morning, Julie. The bathroom is over there. Do you need any help?"

"No. 'Course not."

Just as well, Carissa thought as she stretched and glanced at the clock. Her only experience with children had been several years ago when she'd looked after a friend's son and daughter while the parents attended an out-of-town funeral. She hadn't learned enough in those two days to develop any maternal instincts, even if she had any.

It was seven o'clock, according to Naomi's clock radio. She supposed she'd have to get up, but she didn't face the day with any enthusiasm. She wondered how Paul had spent the night.

"You got enough water to flush?" Julie called from the bathroom.

"Yes," Carissa answered quickly. She had just swung her feet over the side of the bed, when, carrying the teddy bear, Lauren walked into the bedroom.

"Hurry up, Julie. It's my turn," Lauren whined.

"Just washing my hands. Okay?" Julie answered her sister.

"How are you this morning, Lauren?" Carissa asked.

"Not very good. I had bad dreams."

Could Lauren's dreams be any worse than the reality of their lives? A sick mother, and a father who'd deserted them. And not enough water to flush! Considering the terrible life these children had experienced, Carissa decided her childhood could have been much worse.

She or Paul would have to notify the police. But what would happen to the kids if they were put in state custody?

"Is it all right if I slip into the bathroom first, Lauren?" Carissa asked. "Then I can go and prepare breakfast."

The child nodded, a resigned expression on her face. Seemingly timid, Lauren had probably been in second place all of her life.

Deciding a shower would have to wait, Carissa hurriedly washed her face and hands. She slipped into a warm robe, wrapped it securely around her body and put on some fleece-lined slippers.

"It's your turn now, Lauren. Thanks for waiting."

"You sure look pretty," Lauren said. "Our mom used to be pretty, too."

Carissa patted Lauren's shoulder without speaking. She hardly knew what to say to these children.

Julie was in the adjoining bedroom making her bed, and Carissa said, "Come down when you're ready. I'll see about some breakfast."

"Okay," Julie said cheerfully, as if she didn't have a care in the world.

Paul was sprawled on the recliner, still in the dark-blue pajamas he'd been wearing last night when he'd come to her rescue. Not wanting to disturb him, she tiptoed toward the kitchen.

"Good morning," he said, shifting to a sitting position.

"Oh, I didn't know you were awake," Carissa said. "Sorry to disturb you. I thought you were sleeping in the bedroom."

He pushed his hands through his disheveled brown hair and shook his head groggily. "I decided that I couldn't hear what was going on if I was in the bedroom. I also took the precaution of piling some things in front of the door, in case our visitors tried to escape. I've known that trick to work," he said, with a quirk of his heavy eyebrows.

That brought a blush to her face.

His glance quickly surveyed her appearance. The blue fleece robe deepened the tint of her eyes. The belt, tied snugly around her middle, emphasized a slim waist that flowed into shapely hips. For the first time, Paul realized what a dainty, beautiful woman Carissa was. His scrutiny must have embarrassed Carissa, because her blush deepened to scarlet.

"My bedroom and bath have been taken over by two kids," Carissa said. "I didn't have enough privacy to get out of my nightclothes. You'll have to excuse my appearance."

"If I looked that good in a robe, I'd never put on pants and shirts," he said.

Carissa hadn't thought her face could get any redder, but she was sure it had.

Paul followed her into the kitchen and prepared the coffeepot. "If you're okay with it, as soon as we've eaten, I'm going to contact Justin. He may already know about our fugitives. The AMBER alert is active in most states now. Justin has a family of his own, and he'll be sympathetic to the kids' situation, but he'll also know the best move to make."

"I feel sorry for them, but we could be accused of kidnapping if we don't notify the authorities right away."

"My opinion, too. I'll go to my apartment, shower

and dress while you finish breakfast. I'll call for Alex on my way out. I'm worried about this—we need to get it resolved.''

Paul opened the door leading to the basement and called, ''Alex, time to get up. Breakfast will be ready soon.''

Three grim-faced children huddled together on the sofa as they awaited the arrival of Yuletide's police chief. Paul had taken care of the breakfast dishes while Carissa showered and dressed in winter-white sweats.

The sound of a squad car whizzing up the road made Carissa wonder if Justin Townsend ever observed the speed limit. When the knock came at the door, Paul opened it for the police officer. On the phone earlier, Paul simply told Justin they had a problem and asked him to come to the house as soon as possible.

''Hiya!'' Justin said jovially as he entered the room. ''So you're the one standing on your feet now, Paul. Don't tell me you've knocked Miss Whitmore down.''

Paul motioned toward the couch, and Justin's eyes narrowed speculatively when he saw the children.

''Carissa and I are all right,'' Paul said. ''But we do have company. Sit down.''

Taking a sharp breath, Justin dropped heavily into the nearest chair. With an incredulous glance at the kids and then at Paul, the chief demanded, "What's going on?"

Briefly, Paul explained the events of the previous night and what he knew about the children. He ended by asking, "Have you had any communication about three runaways?"

"Nary a thing," Justin said. "And we get updates every day." He turned to the children. "Where's your home?" he demanded.

The girls were obviously frightened, and Alex must have been, too, for a vein throbbed noticeably in his forehead and panic was mirrored in his brown eyes. But his voice was steady when he said, "We don't have a home."

"All right," Justin continued. "Let's get at it another way. Where did you live before you didn't have a home?"

A stubborn set to his jaw, Alex shook his head.

Paul and Justin exchanged glances. With a shrug of his broad shoulders, Paul gestured in a sweeping manner with his right arm.

"That's the reaction we've had from them."

"What if I tell you I'm going to put you in jail?" Justin said severely, and Carissa gasped.

"That's okay," Alex said belligerently. "We'd get somethin' to eat, we'd be together and we'd be warm. That's all we want."

"Mommy asked Alex to look after us," Julie said, moving close to her brother. "And he's been tryin' to."

Justin looked as baffled as Carissa and Paul had felt when they'd discovered the kids in the house.

"The children were going to be separated into the homes of different relatives after their mother's death," Carissa explained. "That's the reason they ran away."

"They're too young to make decisions like that," Justin protested.

"I know that," Paul said. "And so do you. But we've gathered that the kids have been pretty much on their own and taking care of their sick mother for over a year. They still think they can manage alone."

Justin lifted himself out of the chair. "Well, I'll make a few discreet inquiries and see what I can learn." He scratched his head. "But what am I going to do with them now?" he added.

The kids seemed to cringe, and their eyes surveyed the three adults as they waited for judgment to be passed on them. Carissa closed her eyes against the entreaty she saw in their grief-pinched faces, and again her own miserable childhood passed through her mind.

"They can stay here with me until you do some investigating," Carissa said.

"That doesn't seem right," Justin protested. "You're on vacation. I can probably find a place for them in town."

Carissa looked for a moment at the children, and her glance briefly grazed Paul's face in passing.

"I thought I came to Yuletide for a vacation, but

maybe God had some other reason in mind. I've not been His most obedient follower, but for the past twenty years, I've never doubted that God was masterminding my life. If He hadn't been, with my limitations, I wouldn't have made it.'' She glanced again at the children. ''I thought I'd retired and could take it easy the rest of my life. This may be a test to show me that I'm not ready for retirement.''

Paul's expression held a mixture of admiration and concern. ''It shouldn't be more than a few days,'' he said.

''I'm not sure I should agree to this,'' Justin said. ''Naomi won't like having you move someone else into her house.''

''I hadn't thought of that,'' Carissa said. ''Our agreement didn't provide for this situation. But as Paul mentioned, it won't be more than a few days.''

The children had listened in silence as the adults discussed their fate. Now Julie took matters into her own hands by running to Paul and grabbing him around the knees.

''I want to stay here with you, Uncle Paul,'' she said, and compassionately, Paul lifted her and held her in his arms. He was momentarily speechless— he'd never been called ''Uncle Paul.''

Though Justin was visibly touched by the plight of the children, nevertheless, he looked at Alex and said sternly, ''Now, young man, I want some straight answers out of you. Are you in any trouble with the law? Have you broken into any other houses?''

Alex stood as if he were a prisoner before the bench. "No, sir. We wouldn't have come into *this* house, except our money was all gone. I didn't know what else to do. We wouldn't have run away, but I'd heard our neighbors talking. No one wanted us, and if we'd gone on welfare, we might have been sent anywhere. We'd lost everything else—we didn't want to lose each other."

Justin cleared his throat huskily, pulled out a big red handkerchief and blew his nose.

Lauren was crying piteously, her glasses steamed up by her tears. Carissa, almost in tears herself, moved to the couch and gathered the girl into her arms.

Still holding Julie, Paul said to Justin, "I'll give Carissa a hand. I'm going to be home for a few weeks. I'll clear it with Naomi."

Justin ambled toward the door. "It's good of you two to take on this responsibility." And to Alex, who was still standing ramrod straight, he said, "Relax, kid. I'll do the best I can for you."

When the door closed behind Justin, Lauren peered up at Carissa with reddened eyes. "Does that mean we can stay with you?"

"For the time being, at least."

"Do you have any little girls of your own?"

"No, and I don't know anything about little girls. You'll have to help me."

"We will," Julie said, still in the shelter of Paul's arms. "What're we going to call you?"

Carissa pondered the question. Paul was apparently going to be called "uncle." She really didn't want to become an aunt to the children, so she said, "Miss Carissa should be all right."

Julie tried to twist her tongue around those words but she couldn't handle Carissa.

"What about Miss Cara?" Paul asked.

"Miss Cara," Julie said, proud of getting it right the first time. "We'll call you Miss Cara."

In her close contact with Lauren, Carissa had detected a distinct body odor. The children probably hadn't bathed for weeks. "The first thing is for you to have a bath and put on clean clothes."

"We didn't bring many clothes, and they're all dirty," Alex said.

Carissa sighed. After having no one but herself to look after for years, Carissa wondered if she could possibly take on the responsibility of three children.

Paul noticed that Carissa's body was as taut as a bowstring, and a pensive expression darkened her blue eyes. She licked her lips nervously. Paul set Julie on the floor and knelt by the couch where Carissa was sitting.

Taking her hand, he said, "It'll work out all right. The washer and dryer are in the basement, so Alex and I will sort their clothes and do the laundry while you take care of the girls' baths. We'll get along."

"I feel completely inadequate, but I'll do the best I can." She stood and reached out a hand to the girls. "Come on, Julie and Lauren."

Since there was a shower stall as well as a tub in Carissa's private bathroom, the girls bathed at the same time. The clothes they removed were odorous, and Carissa said, "I'll find a blanket for you to put on until Paul and Alex have clean clothes ready. You can sit and watch TV until then."

While in the other room searching for blankets, Carissa noticed that Lauren hadn't made her bed. She stopped to spread the blankets and stopped short. There was a wet spot in the middle. She had a bed wetter on her hands!

Appalled, Carissa pulled the offending covers from the bed, and breathed a sigh of relief when she saw a protective plastic cover over the mattress. At least the whole bed wasn't ruined. But what was she going to do?

Was she violating her agreement with Naomi to let the children stay, even for a few days? She would be responsible for any damage—but that was hardly the point. What was the ethical thing to do? How would she feel if Naomi took three vagrant children into her Florida condo?

When their baths were finished, she gave a blanket to each of the girls and turned on the television hanging on the wall facing Naomi's bed. Julie's tight ringlets only needed to be brushed, but Carissa struggled to comb Lauren's long hair and braid it.

"You stay here until your clothes have dried," Carissa said. "I'll take these clothes to be washed." Carissa had a keen sense of smell, and she held her breath as she picked up the girls' clothes and the soiled sheets and took them to the basement.

Paul had found a checkers set and, while they waited for the clothes to dry, he and Alex were sitting at a small table in the game room shoving the red and black disks across a board. Carissa passed them and peered into the furnace room, admiring the ingenuity of the children in providing for themselves. They'd apparently found two cots, which the girls had occupied, and Alex's bed had been laid on some cushions that Naomi probably used on the porch furniture during the summer. They would have been comfortable enough, but how they expected to spend the winter here, Carissa couldn't comprehend.

"Where are my sisters?" Alex asked.

"Wrapped in blankets, lying on my bed, watching television. A life of ease," she said, with a grimace in Paul's direction.

The washer was still on but a buzzer indicated that the clothes in the dryer were ready. When Paul started to get up from the checker game, Carissa said, "I'll fold the clothes. Go ahead and play."

Paul had sorted the clothing by color, so there were three small loads to wash. The poor quality of the worn clothing further attested to the poverty the children had experienced. When the washer finished, Carissa emptied its contents into the dryer and put the remaining clothes and sheets in the washer.

"After Lauren and Julie have dressed, let's go outside and play in the snow,'' she said. ''I didn't come to New York to spend my time inside.''

''Sounds like a good idea,'' Paul said. ''We'll be upstairs as soon as the clothes are washed and dry.''

The children's shoes and clothes weren't warm enough for them to stay outside long, but they took a brisk walk along the lakeshore. They even ventured out to one of the fishermen's huts and waited expectantly, but the man didn't catch anything while they watched.

The five of them engaged in a snowball fight, and even though the females outnumbered the males, Alex and Paul were formidable opponents. When Paul tossed a snowball that exploded in Carissa's face, she shouted, ''I give up,'' and hurried inside the house.

Thinking he might have hurt her, Paul said, ''Go ahead and play. I'll see if Carissa is okay.''

Carissa was wiping the snow from her face when Paul entered the kitchen. Her glowing eyes indicated that she was all right, but Paul said solicitously, ''I didn't intend such a direct hit. Are you hurt?''

''Nothing except my pride,'' she said with a laugh.

''Fortunately this snow is light. It doesn't pack well.''

Carissa looked out the window toward where the children were trying to make a snowman. ''They seemed almost happy while we were playing. Paul, I feel so sorry for them, but I'm ill-prepared to deal with three orphan children.''

"You're doing great," he said reassuringly. "I have a strange feeling about this situation, as if God is giving us an opportunity to help. If He's orchestrating what we're doing, we can't fail."

Chapter Six

Paul spent the rest of the morning repairing the lock on the rear door. Then, early that afternoon, help arrived in the guise of Belva Townsend, Justin's wife. Belva was stocky of build, and her features were pleasant but not pretty. She had a brusque manner, but five minutes in her presence and Carissa's burden about the children lifted considerably. She didn't know what to do, Belva obviously did.

After Paul introduced Belva and Carissa, Belva said, "I came to have a look at these kids and see what they need."

"Just about everything," Paul told her. "They have one pair of well-worn shoes each. And their other clothing is sparse."

"I'll take them shopping this afternoon," Carissa said.

"I doubt you'll have to buy anything," Belva said.

She lined the children up and observed them closely, talking about them as if they weren't present. "My boys have outgrown clothes that I think Alex can wear. And no doubt I can get many things for the girls from my neighbors. We also have a clothing bank at the church. I'll be back this evening with some things. Don't buy anything yet."

"Say, Belva," Paul said, "we've been wondering if any Christmas celebrations are planned. Both Carissa and I would like to experience an old-time Christmas again."

Belva helped herself to one of the cheese cubes left over from lunch. "Yuletide has never revived the large celebrations like we used to have. A few people decorate their homes and lawns, but old-timers, who still remember the past, can't get enthused about celebrating."

"Seems to me it's time to forget the past," Paul said.

"You may be right," Belva agreed. "But don't talk to me—take up your grievances with the town council."

With a cheery wave of her arm, Belva trotted down the porch steps and was gone. Her visit hadn't lasted fifteen minutes.

"Sorta feel like I've been in a blitzkrieg," Carissa said with a laugh. However, Belva's matter-of-fact approach to the situation had done a lot to calm her spirits.

"Belva can be a bit abrupt," Paul agreed. "But she has a heart of gold."

True to her word, several hours later, Belva returned with fleece-lined parkas, sweatpants and shirts for the children. She brought some books and a doll for Julie. As they looked at the books and modeled their new clothes, the children seemed happy, though occasionally, a bleak expression appeared in Alex's and Lauren's eyes.

Feeling that the children were content in their new surroundings, Paul didn't think it was necessary to guard them, so that night he went to bed in his sister's room.

Long after the household was quiet, bundled in her heaviest garments, Carissa crept down the stairs. She ventured out on the deck that Paul had swept clear of snow, and sat on a bench.

A bright moon hung over the evergreen trees, and a soft breeze wafted from the lake. The night was cold and still. In such a peaceful setting, Carissa should have been as calm as the atmosphere, but her thoughts were rioting.

She had wanted to remember the Christmases of old, but she hadn't expected to be plunged into a roller-coaster return of thoughts of her unhappy childhood. The past few days had awakened recollections of her past that she had tried in vain to forget.

In a large city, her forlorn childhood wouldn't have caused a ripple, but in a town of five hundred people, no one had any secrets. Except for the members of her grandmother's church, people in town had shunned her. Because her mother had an unsavory reputation, the townspeople had labeled Carissa with the same immoral qualities, expecting her to follow in her mother's footsteps. No decent boy had ever asked her for a date, and only a few girls befriended her—children who were also ostracized for one reason or another. Carissa hadn't been an outgoing child, and she'd made no overtures of friendship to others. She'd feared rejection then, and she still did.

She would have liked to marry and have children, but when she didn't even know who her father was, what kind of heritage would she have passed to her offspring? Any of her mother's partners could have fathered her.

She'd loved her mother devotedly, but after her death, Carissa had learned about her lifestyle and had come to resent her. She blamed her mother for bringing her into the world under such a cloud, and she didn't want children who would someday resent her for passing on a sordid ancestry to them.

She was past child-bearing age now, however, so what harm would there be in finding happiness with a husband? Carissa was a little surprised at herself.

Once she'd made up her mind years ago to remain single, she'd never thought about marriage, so why this sudden remorse that she'd remained single? Could it be the children who'd suddenly come into her life? Or was it Paul who'd triggered her desire for wedded bliss?

She feared that was the reason. During her youth, she'd missed a father figure in her life. The only close male relative who'd influenced her at all was an uncle. He was kind to her, but he had a houseful of his own kids and didn't have enough time to take Carissa under his wing.

But in those youthful days before she'd decided never to marry, she'd envisioned the kind of man she wanted to marry. Carissa had become an introvert through necessity, so she'd wanted a husband who was a friendly person, one who'd smile often, one with a strong, physical body that belied the tenderness that he exhibited so readily. And she'd wanted a man who would love her without reservation, one who would be able to understand her fears, one whose presence would calm her spirits and stir her emotions. Only a few hours in Paul's presence and she knew he exemplified all the characteristics of her dream man.

She hadn't heard a sound, but suddenly she sensed that she was no longer alone, and knew Paul had joined her. How was it possible to become so quickly attuned to this man that she could actually perceive his presence without seeing or hearing him?

"You couldn't sleep, either?" she asked.

Paul moved forward to stand near Carissa. He'd been watching her for several minutes. He hadn't made a sound, so he wondered how she could have known he was there.

"No. I'm still having a problem with jet lag."

He wasn't being exactly truthful, because actually, he'd been thinking about Carissa when he'd heard her come downstairs. After Jennifer Pruett had jilted him twenty years ago, Paul had successfully stifled any interest in women. It wasn't really difficult, for Jennifer had hurt him so badly that he didn't want another woman in his life. Since that time, he'd seldom given any woman a second thought. So what attracted him to Carissa?

Perhaps it was because, in spite of her outward appearance of success, he sensed that Carissa experienced much inner turmoil. Behind her facade of self-assurance, he sensed a little girl's wistfulness in her remote, and sometimes mysterious, smile. He'd been alone for years because he wanted it that way. Carissa was obviously alone, too, but he suspected that her natural tendency was to want people.

She was a small, slender woman with a delicate, fragile body. He could easily span her waist with his hands. But remembering the way she'd flinched when he'd touched her on the shoulder, Paul knew it would be a long time, if ever, before he could put his hands around her waist. And why should he want to?

"I don't even have that excuse," Carissa commented, turning to face him as he closed the door.

Paul had been so immersed in his thoughts that,

for a moment, he couldn't remember what they were talking about.

"Oh, no jet lag? What's the problem, then?"

"I can't get the kids out of my mind. I want to do right by them, but I'm reluctant to take on this responsibility."

"Don't you like kids?"

Carissa laughed shortly. Not like kids when she'd recently signed a $200,000 check to help fund a shelter for abandoned children?

"That's hardly the point. I have a soft spot in my heart for children, especially orphaned ones like our three guests, but I'm uncomfortable about bringing them into Naomi's house. Besides, it seems to be the ethical thing to turn them over to the authorities."

"Well, Justin is working on that. And I'll call Naomi today and clear it with her."

Paul wore a parka over his pajamas, and his feet were in slippers. He shivered and pulled the parka closer to his body.

"You'll freeze out here with so few clothes on. I'm ready to go in, anyway. Sorry I disturbed your rest. I just had to deal with some of my frustrations," she said.

"Do you think you'll sleep now?"

"I should be able to," she said, but Paul was aware of the concern in her eyes. He opened the door and stood aside to let Carissa into the room.

Paul figured she'd take her worries to bed with her. But there was a limit to what he could do, so he returned to the bedroom and closed the door, as Carissa headed toward the stairs.

Carissa and Paul were lingering over their coffee when Justin and Belva came the next morning. The children were still sleeping, so Carissa invited the couple to join them for coffee. Paul got cups while Carissa poured the hot beverage.

Justin said, "I can't turn up a thing on those kids. It's inconceivable in this day of mass communication that three kids can disappear without somebody looking for them."

"You could put their pictures on the Internet and you'd soon find out who they are and where they came from," Paul said.

"I know, and I'll probably do that, but we have complications." He darted a look at his wife, and Carissa had the feeling that Justin was a mite henpecked.

"As you know, Paul," Justin continued, "Yuletide is a small town and news travels fast. By now, everyone in town knows about these three kids. I've had a half dozen phone calls or so asking me not to relocate the children until after Christmas."

"Yuletide's citizens are deluding themselves into believing that these children have been sent to us to give us an opportunity to redeem ourselves," said Belva.

"Maybe it isn't a delusion," Paul said.

Half annoyed that she couldn't follow the gist of

their conversation, Carissa remembered what Paul had told her two nights ago. "Oh, now I understand. They're tying the present situation to the Christmas Eve tragedy of the past."

"That's right," Justin said. "People are begging me not to do anything until after Christmas. The mayor wants the town to adopt them as our special guests for the next few weeks. Even the pastor of Bethel Church stopped by the office last night, suggesting that the children might give us a second chance to show our generosity and faith."

"But can't you get into a lot of trouble by not trying to find out whose children they are?" Paul asked.

Justin slanted an uneasy look toward his wife, who took a sip of coffee, seemingly oblivious to his gaze.

"But I might get into a lot more trouble if I don't do what the Yuletide citizens want me to do. Besides, I *am* trying to find out who the kids are."

When Belva didn't comment, Justin asked, "What do the two of you think about it? You're more involved than anyone else."

Paul's eyes registered concern when he looked at Carissa. He hadn't anticipated spending his vacation in this manner, but he was willing to help out. And what about his visit with Naomi? He wouldn't go to Florida and leave Carissa with the responsibility.

"You'd expect us to be the children's guardians until after Christmas?" he asked Justin.

"Others in town would be willing to give them a

home,'' Belva said, ''but I'm not sure anyone can take all three of them.''

''Then they'd be separated!'' Carissa said. ''That's what they were trying to avoid when they ran away.''

She moved from the table to stand in front of the window. Hoarfrost decorated the windowpane in lacy, geometric patterns. Ice fishermen already huddled over holes in the lake. As she watched, one man pulled a foot-long fish from the frigid water.

Carissa saw the scenery, but her thoughts were far removed from the beauty of the winter morning. For years she'd been a heavy contributor to children's charities—but was God now giving her the opportunity to donate hands-on help to children whose needs exceeded hers as a child?

She'd been anticipating two months of inactivity, and deep down in her heart, Carissa didn't want to take on this responsibility. She hadn't been in Yuletide a week, and if she assumed the care of these children until after Christmas, over half of her time there would be gone. And what about her quest for Christmas? She couldn't continue that as long as she was playing mother.

Or was God giving her the opportunity to find Christmas through the three children?

''Do unto others as you would have them do unto you.'' The Scripture verse she'd learned as a child flashed into her mind.

Why couldn't she put memories of her childhood behind her? She'd buried her past while she built up

Cara Fashions, so why did her past intrude upon her thoughts now? Obviously, she hadn't dealt with the youthful heartaches she'd experienced, or she would be able to forget them.

"If Paul can get Naomi's okay, I'll look after the kids," she said, her heart speaking instead of her head. She wasn't sure what she was getting into.

"Good!" Belva said, a full smile lighting her irregular features. "I've already talked with the teachers, and the children will be welcome to come to school." She stood up. "Come, love," she said to her husband. "We have lots of things to do. Thanks for the coffee."

"I still think it's too big a risk for all of us to take," Paul said, as Justin pushed back from the table. "We don't know that these kids are even telling us the truth. They may have a family looking for them."

"You don't really believe that, do you?" Justin asked.

"No," Paul said slowly, and he looked at Carissa's tense features. "But I know Carissa is reluctant, and she'll be bearing the brunt of this because they'll be living in her house. She has a lot at stake."

With her accumulated wealth, Carissa realized that she'd be ripe for plucking if anyone wanted to sue her. But she remembered what her grandmother had said the day she started to Florida: "It's a big change for you, my dear, but you'll never be happy living in this town. Always remember God's promise, 'The

Lord is my helper; I will not be afraid. What can man do to me?''"

"If I thought of myself, I couldn't do this," she said. "For some reason, God sent these children to this house when I was here to receive them. If I told you I wasn't afraid, I'd be lying. I don't know anything about cooking for children or buying their clothes."

"Listen, my dear," Belva said. "I've raised five kids. If you need any help, I'm as close as the telephone. And don't you worry about clothing. The church's clothing bank has good items. You bring the children in at two o'clock this afternoon, and we'll outfit them in whatever else they need."

When the door closed behind the Townsends, Paul laughed softly. "Belva has always liked to be in charge of things," he said, "but she will be a source of wisdom to us."

"Well, we're committed. What do we do now?"

"Let's get the kids out of bed and tell them about the town's plans for them."

Carissa said, "I dread checking Lauren's bed—she's apparently a bed wetter. I hoped the first night's incident was caused by stress, but if the bed-wetting persists, I'll have to talk to Belva about it. I won't ruin Naomi's furniture."

"Which reminds me—I have to talk to Naomi. I'll go to the apartment and call her."

"Please be candid with me. If she doesn't want

the children in the house, I'll take them to a motel and keep them.''

"I know my sister, and she'll understand the situation. But we'd better resolve the matter of where I'm going to live. If you're uncomfortable about staying alone with the children, I'll continue to sleep in Naomi's room.''

With her gaze downcast, Carissa wondered which situation would make her more uncomfortable. She was uneasy about being in the house alone with the kids. They didn't seem to be dangerous, but the media often carried reports of children who were violent.

But was it wise to share a house with Paul, when his every movement demonstrated his masculine attractiveness? She had sensed something exceptional about him from the very beginning, as if the qualities she'd always admired in men were all wrapped up in one bundle, Paul Spencer. Physically and emotionally, she was aware of his every move—his ready sense of humor, the lurking smile in his eyes, his warmheartedness, and the one lock of hair that consistently fell over his forehead. It wasn't worry over the children that had kept her awake last night, but Paul's presence in the house.

She tried to force her swirling emotions into order. For years she'd denied herself the companionship of any man. And suddenly the thought that had been nagging for entrance into her mind surged forward. She was five years older than Paul—too much of an age difference to become more to him than a friend. She'd never approved of women who married men younger than themselves. She'd have to be careful she didn't reveal any of her thoughts to Paul, which would be embarrassing to both of them.

Annoyed that she was again thinking of marriage, she turned to Paul, hoping that her face didn't reveal the tumult of her thoughts.

"If you don't mind, I'd prefer it if you'd stay in the house with us. But you have to go to see Naomi, so don't let my hang-ups prevent you from going to Florida. If you stay here a few days, I'll be more accustomed to the kids by then."

"I would like to see Naomi, but I won't leave you with all this responsibility. I committed to watching out for the children as much as you did. I'll find time to visit my sister."

Paul shifted his eyes from her intense expression, afraid to contemplate why he craved Carissa's company. He could plead the necessity of helping with the children, but was that the real reason he intended to spend Christmas in Yuletide?

Chapter Seven

Overjoyed that they were going to stay with Paul and Carissa, Lauren and Julie enthusiastically jumped into Carissa's SUV to go into town. Paul noticed that Alex was uneasy, and he glanced often from side to side. When they reached the church—a stone structure built from native materials and topped by a tall steeple—Paul drew Alex to one side.

"Alex, we aren't trying to trap you. Unless something else turns up, you can stay with Carissa and me until after Christmas."

Alex shuffled his feet in the light dusting of snow that had fallen the night before.

"So be honest with me. Is there somebody looking for you?"

"I don't think so. I can't tell you anything else, because I want to keep my sisters together like Mom said. She was an adopted kid, and she didn't have any idea whether she had any sisters or brothers. My aunts and uncles are all on my father's side. If they took us, they'd just do it so they could get state money for giving us a home. I promised Mom I'd look out for the girls.''

Paul privately thought that his mother had laid a heavy burden on the back of a fourteen-year-old. He put his arm around Alex's shoulders. ''We'll help you keep your promise. Come on inside, and we'll find some more clothes.''

Belva met them in the church basement and introduced the church's pastor, Philip Erskine. The pastor was a young man who'd come to Yuletide three years ago.

''If you'll allow Belva to take care of the children's needs, I'd like to talk to you in my office,'' Philip said to Carissa and Paul.

Knowing the children's insecurity, Carissa said, ''Is that okay with you, kids? Belva will show you around the clothing room.''

''Where you gonna be?'' Lauren said fearfully.

Pastor Erskine pointed to a door directly across the hall from the room that held the clothing. ''That's my office. You can come in with us when you're finished. We'll leave the door open.''

''Remember, Belva,'' Carissa said. ''I'll purchase anything they need, but you'll have to tell me what to buy.''

Belva nodded. ''We'll see what's available here in their sizes.''

Inviting them to sit, Pastor Erskine said, "This is my second Christmas in Yuletide. It's inconceivable to me that these people won't celebrate the birth of Jesus in their homes or the church. I don't believe that God has withdrawn His blessing from their town because of what happened twenty-five years ago, but I can't convince my congregation."

With a smile, he continued. "If the local citizens feel that they've been given a chance to help the children and atone for that previous oversight, I believe I should take advantage of it. I'm not above exploiting that superstition to accomplish what I want."

"Which is to have the town celebrate Christmas?" Paul said with a laugh.

"Right! Chief Townsend told me this morning that the two of you wanted to revive an old-time Christmas in Yuletide. Will you help me?"

Carissa and Paul exchanged glances. A faint light sparkled in the depths of Carissa's blue eyes, and Paul knew she was willing to do what the pastor asked.

"Suits me," Paul said, "but we don't have much time."

"So we must start right away," the pastor said. "I'll call a meeting of some of the town's influential people tonight at seven. Will you come?"

"I wouldn't like to leave the children alone—they might run away," Carissa said.

"Tonight is our monthly youth rally with activities

for all ages. Your children could profit by attending the meeting.''

Surprised at herself because she'd made all her decisions since she'd been on her own, Carissa looked to Paul for an answer.

''I'm willing,'' he said. ''For one thing, it will give the kids some diversion. Carissa and I aren't exactly gifted in entertaining children.'' He glanced in Carissa's direction. ''All right?''

''Yes. We'll be here tonight.''

Twelve people attended the meeting, and due to an intense spirit of cooperation, plans were formulated quickly.

''We've got our work cut out for us if we plan on getting all of these things done in the next two weeks,'' Paul said as they were driving home. ''The decorations should be up now, so people from out of town can come to see them.''

''If we extend the time until after the first of the year, tourists will have the opportunity to stop by,'' Carissa added. ''Especially if the mayor gets coverage in big-city newspapers.''

The committee had decided that within the next week, the stores would be decorated, and a large spruce tree, in a vacant lot near City Hall, would be covered with colored lights. The pastor had referred to a catalog featuring lighted commercial displays, wishing they could erect an exhibition along the lakefront.

When he bemoaned the fact that even a modest display would cost five thousand dollars, Carissa had said, "I'll pay for the display. Go ahead and order what you need."

All heads had turned in her direction, and she wished she'd waited until later to tell the pastor. Normally, she made her charitable contributions more discreetly.

"That's good of you, Miss Whitmore." Pastor Erskine had surveyed the group seated in his small office. "But is there time to get these things and have them erected?"

The pastor's secretary had said, "I looked through that catalog, and the company sends representatives to erect the displays and put them into operation."

Embarrassed when, at the close of the meeting, several of the people thanked her warmly for contributing the money for the light display, Carissa had wished again that she hadn't made her donation public. Paul had made no comment one way or another.

On the way home, as Carissa expertly handled her vehicle on the slippery roads, Paul realized that he had apparently been the only one who wasn't pleased about Carissa's generous offer. He should have complimented her, too, but he was wary of people, and especially women, who had a lot of money. Although Jennifer had insisted she loved him, she'd jilted him because he was poor. When she'd had the opportunity to marry a rich man, Jennifer had chosen money over her love for Paul.

Carissa had noticed that Paul seemed to be the only one at the meeting not overjoyed that the town would have a light display. And even as they talked in the car, she wondered why he didn't mention her offer.

"You kids have a good time?" he asked the children, as Carissa parked, and the kids tumbled out of the SUV.

Julie grabbed Paul's hand and held up a Christmas ornament she'd made. "Look, Uncle Paul. The teacher told us to put this on our tree."

"Are we gonna have a Christmas tree?" Lauren asked. "We couldn't have one last year."

Carissa looked to Paul for that decision, too, and he answered easily enough, although she sensed his preoccupation.

"Of course we'll have a tree. We can cut one on the hill behind the house."

"What did your group do?" Carissa asked Alex as they entered the house.

"Played games. My team got the Ping-Pong trophy for the most wins. We played Bingo, too. I won three candy bars. Here, girls," he said, handing a bar to each of his sisters.

"Maybe we'd better save ours until tomorrow," Lauren said, when Julie started opening the package.

Carissa couldn't determine whether Lauren was concerned because they shouldn't eat chocolate at bedtime, or whether she'd developed the habit of hoarding because of the scarcity of food in their home. Wondering how many times these children had gone to bed hungry, Carissa said, "Why don't you eat half of the candy now and keep the rest until tomorrow?"

"We had 'freshments at the church," Julie admitted. "And Mommy didn't want us to eat before bedtime."

"Then, by all means, save the candy until tomorrow."

The fragrance of coffee awakened Carissa the next morning. She'd slept well in spite of her concern over Paul's attitude last night. When she tried to pinpoint when he'd changed, she traced it to the time she'd volunteered to pay for the light display. Did he think she was flaunting her money? After being so poor through her childhood and feeling inferior to most of the other children in her school, Carissa had made an effort not to offend anyone with her prosperity.

She peered into the other bedroom. Lauren and Julie were still sleeping, so Carissa closed the door between the rooms. She showered and dressed in jeans and a turtleneck sweater before going downstairs.

Paul was busy in the kitchen. He'd prepared a pitcher of frozen orange juice. Sausage patties were laid out ready for the microwave, and he was mixing something in a bowl.

"You're energetic this morning," Carissa said

when she entered the kitchen. "Are you making a cake?"

He grinned at her in his usual way, saying, "This is pancake batter. I decided we should have something besides sweet rolls this morning. Do you like pancakes?"

"Very much, but I get mine from the freezer section in the grocery store, then pop them in the microwave. I haven't had homemade pancakes since I lived with my grandmother. It isn't much fun to cook for one person."

"I'm no fancy cook, but I like to putter around the kitchen."

"Good!" Carissa said, a teasing quality in her voice. "Then, you can be the cook for this joint venture we've taken on."

"Suits me! You can take care of any homework that has to be supervised, as well as discipline the kids."

"I'll pass on that, too," Carissa said. "I believe parents should work as a team in disciplining their children. I grew up in an all-female household, and I always felt I'd missed a lot by not having some male influence."

"What happened to your father?" Paul asked.

"Well, about that…" Carissa started. At the strain in her voice, Paul looked at her questioningly. Before she could finish, Alex walked into the kitchen.

"Hey!" he said. "I smell food."

"And good food, too," Carissa said, obviously relieved that Alex had interrupted them. "I'll see if Julie and Lauren are out of bed."

"What can I do to help?" Alex asked Paul as Carissa turned toward the steps.

She was tormented by confusing emotions. Why did she find it so difficult to talk about her teen years?

She hadn't wanted any of her business associates to know of her past, and she'd never told anyone about her sordid family background. When she left Minnesota at eighteen, Carissa had believed that her unsavory past would follow her, but miraculously, it hadn't. Therefore, for over twenty years, she'd been spared talking about that period of her life. If Alex hadn't walked in, would she have told Paul?

Carissa supervised the girls while they showered and changed into some of the clothes they'd gotten at the clothing bank. She couldn't imagine that two sisters could have such opposite personalities. Julie only took a few minutes to decide what clothes she wanted to wear, and dressed quickly without much supervision from Carissa.

Lauren, on the other hand, chose one shirt, but when she put it on, she started crying. "Miss Cara, Julie's clothes are all prettier than mine."

"But, Lauren," Carissa said, "you had the opportunity to choose what things you wanted."

"Yes, but the clothes in my size weren't very pretty."

"Of course they are," Carissa said. She turned

Lauren to face the mirror. "The brown in this shirt is the color of your hair, and these little yellow stripes reflect the golden flecks in your eyes. I think you made a great choice."

"Do you *really* think so?" Julie asked worriedly.

"Yes, I do. And let's leave your hair hanging over your shoulders instead of braiding it today. You have such pretty, soft hair, it's a shame to braid it."

"Julie's hair is curly."

"It's pretty, too, but not any prettier than yours. Stop comparing yourself to Julie. You're different girls, so you should be what God made *you* to be."

"Oh!" Lauren said, and reached her hand to touch Carissa's cheek.

Carissa blinked away the unaccustomed moisture in her eyes. Taking Lauren's hand, she said, "Let's go for breakfast. Paul has made pancakes with sausages this morning."

Soon after breakfast, Paul herded the three children into his pickup and took them into Yuletide to go to school. Since they'd met children their ages the night before, they didn't seem to mind going to a strange school.

"I'll help decorate the central Christmas tree while I'm in town. I'll stay until school is out—probably at three o'clock. Hope you have a nice, quiet day."

In fact, the house seemed too quiet after they left, and Carissa marveled that a few days had changed her perspective. Without Paul and the children, the silence seemed strange as she straightened the house for the day.

The girls had spread the covers over their beds. Although it was a makeshift effort, after Carissa checked to find that Lauren's sheets were dry, she left the beds alone. She wouldn't take away from the independence they'd learned from their mother.

Carissa had finished tidying the house by mid-morning, and she was restless. She walked along the lakefront for an hour, and then decided to go into Yuletide. She needed to open an account at the local bank, and she thought she might be helpful in decorating the community tree. Did she really have a yen to decorate the tree, or did she want to be where Paul was? If so, it was a new sensation for her to deliberately seek the company of a man.

She arrived at the town hall just as the eight volunteers stopped for lunch. She eyed the twenty-foot-tall spruce tree and the ladders that leaned against it. "Any place for a person who prefers her feet on the ground when she works?"

"We're taking a break now," Paul said. "Come along and eat with us, and then we'll find a job for you."

They went to the café Carissa had visited on her first night in Yuletide. It was the only place to eat in town, except for the restaurant in the lobby of the hotel, and it was crowded.

A decorated pine tree stood in one corner of the room, red candles were placed on each table and

Christmas music mingled with the voices of the diners.

"We should put some outside decorations at the house," she said. "If people are driving around the lake to see the light display, the houses should be attractive, too. Where could we go to buy decorations?"

"There won't be anything in Yuletide," Paul said. "Saratoga Springs would be the closest place. We could go tomorrow and get what we need. I told the kids we'd have a Christmas tree, but since it will be a real one, we shouldn't put it up until a few days before Christmas."

"I couldn't get into the spirit of Christmas in Tampa when the temperature on December twenty-fifth is often in the seventies. I have a two-foot artificial tree that I place on the coffee table in my living room. That's the extent of my decorating. It'll be nice to have an evergreen scent in the house."

"Even the years I've been away from home I've always managed to spend Christmas where there's snow. I've spent several Christmases skiing and skating in the Alps."

They met Pastor Erskine as they left the restaurant. "The lighting company will erect the display a week from today. We can't hope for anything better than that, when our order went in so late. But the manager said that the weeks prior to Christmas are slow for them because their customers usually order months in advance. And I've come up with another idea."

"Uh-oh!" Carissa said, feeling mischievous. "That sounds like more work to me."

"I'd like to have a progressive outdoor nativity pageant. The manger scene could be set up beside the town hall, the shepherds and angels could congregate on one of the hillsides outside town, and the Wise Men could travel into Yuletide from the far side of Lake Mohawk."

"Got any camels?" Paul asked.

Pastor Erskine's face suddenly drooped. "I hadn't thought of that. But we don't have any biblical proof that the Wise Men rode camels. They'll have to walk into town."

"A pageant would be a memorable event," Carissa said. "If you need any help with costumes, let me know. I'm a fashion designer, and I make my creations on my own sewing machine before I send out the patterns to the manufacturers."

"Miss Whitmore, I believe in providence. God must have sent you to Yuletide to help us revive the spirit of Christmas. The town is coming alive again."

Silently, Carissa agreed with him, for more and more, she believed that her choice of Yuletide had not been happenstance.

Chapter Eight

The next week passed quickly. Paul and Carissa made a trip to Saratoga Springs to buy decorations. When each insisted that they'd pay for the items, they finally agreed to split the expenses.

"If this year's observance goes well," Carissa said, "Yuletide will probably throw off its fixation about not celebrating Christmas. Perhaps Naomi can use them for another season."

"I don't know," Paul said. "Naomi sounds like she's having such a good time in Florida. She may never spend another winter in the north."

"Yes, I know. I called yesterday to apologize for the way we were misusing her home, and she said that her New York home was the furthest thing from her mind now."

"I thought a change of scenery would be good for her, but I didn't dream she'd become a new person.

Management of the textile mill was apparently too much for her. She says the staff can handle the work, and she isn't worrying about it. She's made new friends. One man from Wyoming has rented an apartment in the complex where you live, and they've been going to dinner together."

Paul spent the next two days draping the evergreens with strings of lights, and he put icicle lights around the eaves of the house. Carissa started decorating the great room.

Thinking that Naomi might also want to decorate, Carissa telephoned to let Naomi know where her meager supply of Christmas decorations was stored. She made three attempts before she finally caught Naomi at the condo.

"You're an elusive lady," Carissa said. "You must spend all your time at the beach."

"I go walking every morning, but there are so many other things to do. My new friend, John Brewster, and I go to a different restaurant for dinner every night."

"Is he the man from Wyoming?"

"Yes. Since he retired, he's spent the past five winters in Florida."

"I'm happy you're enjoying my place as much as I like yours. Since I'm decorating your house today, I thought you might like to put out some decorations, too. I don't have many things, but you'll find what I do have in my storage area in the basement. The key is on the key ring I left for you. If you want more things, I'll pay for them. I can always use them next year.''

''Thanks, but I probably won't do any decorating. I'm out of the habit now, since we haven't done anything at Yuletide for several years.''

''And, Naomi, if you want to come home for Christmas, please do so. One more person in the house won't be a problem. I'm encouraging Paul to come visit you, but he insists he feels responsible for the children, too. I don't want you to be lonely.''

''I thank you, but I'll be content to stay here. I've made many friends, and we have so much in common that I feel as if they're family. John took me to the large church two blocks west of your condo. They have a Bible class especially for northern people who spend the winter months in Florida. Twenty-three people attended, and we're planning many activities for the holidays. Two of the couples live in RVs, and they've rented the clubhouse at their RV park for a big party. We'll all take food and exchange gifts. And we're planning to take a Caribbean cruise for several days, so I won't even be home on Christmas Day. I'm happier than I've been since my husband died, so don't worry about me being lonely.''

How could Naomi have made friends so quickly— friends she preferred to see more than she did her own brother? But Carissa reflected that she'd also become acquainted with many new people in the past three weeks. In the frenzied rush to bring Christmas to Yuletide, they didn't seem like strangers.

Carissa had bought a wooden nativity scene for the mantel, which she surrounded with pine cones and greenery from the trees around the lake. She placed the wooden key she'd carried in the Christmas pageant when she was a child in a prominent place. Each time she looked at it, Carissa was reminded of her reason for coming to Yuletide. She had ropes of tinsel and red poinsettias to tie around the wooden supports in the great room and on the stair railings.

When Paul came home from taking the children to school on Wednesday morning, Carissa was placing electric candles in the windows. He carried a large paper bag that held several sprigs of a plant with small green leaves and clusters of white berries. With a boyish smile, he handed the plants to Carissa.

"What's that?" she asked.

"Mistletoe! I stopped at the farmer's market for a bag of oranges, and he'd just received a shipment of mistletoe. I thought you could use it for decoration."

Frowning, Carissa said, "I'm not so sure. I've heard that mistletoe berries are poisonous to people. With three kids in the house, I don't want to take any chances."

"I didn't buy this for eating. Haven't you ever heard of kissing under the mistletoe?"

She glanced at Paul questioningly. "I can't see that we'll need it for that purpose, either."

"Oh, you never can tell," he answered. "I think our visitors could benefit from a few hugs and kisses.

They probably haven't had much affection since their mother became sick.''

''Whatever you do with the mistletoe, be sure it's out of reach of the children. And you can take care of the affection, too. God must have left maternal instincts out of my makeup. I'm capable of clothing and sheltering our visitors, but I don't seem to have many hugs and kisses to give.''

And I wonder why you don't, Paul thought. From the tense expression on Carissa's face, he felt sure it was a discussion he couldn't initiate at that time.

They chatted companionably the rest of the morning while Paul tied sprigs of mistletoe not only on the chandelier in the great room, but also on the light over the kitchen table. He inserted some of it in Carissa's mantel decorations. It did look pretty as an extra touch, Carissa thought, but she was uneasy about having the mistletoe in the house. She couldn't decide which disturbed her the most—her concern for the children, or what Paul had said about hugs and kisses.

By noon, the great room was festive, and Carissa stood in the middle to survey their efforts. ''I suppose we should have waited for the children to help decorate,'' she said, ''but I didn't think about it. I'm so used to doing things alone that I can't easily include others. We'll let them help trim the tree. Looks good, doesn't it?''

Carissa had inadvertently stopped beneath the mistletoe-decorated chandelier to admire the room's new look. Watching her, and the look on her face, Paul thought she was an exquisite woman. He moved closer, and, putting his left hand on her shoulder, he pointed up at the mistletoe.

''After all, it is a Christmas tradition,'' he said, and bent his head, meaning to kiss her on the forehead.

Carissa quickly lifted her face, and his lips touched hers in an electric moment. Dazed, her eyes closed, Carissa swayed toward Paul.

After a second's hesitation, when he briefly recalled his long-standing vow to avoid women, he hugged her to him in a delight too profound for words.

His kiss was surprisingly gentle, and Carissa was surprised at her eager response to the touch of his lips. She seemed to be drifting through space, her spirits soaring, filled with an inner excitement that was foreign to her. Then suddenly she remembered! Her eyes flew open. A glint of wonder had transformed Paul's gaze.

Wrenching out of his arms, Carissa pushed Paul away from her. Caught off guard, he stumbled backward and sprawled in a crumpled heap on the couch, mashing the boxes that had held the decorations.

Running toward the stairs, Carissa said in a tearful voice, ''Don't ever touch me again.''

Angered, not only by his own emotional reaction to Carissa, but also by her rejection of his advances, Paul shouted angrily, ''I don't intend to. I'm going to the apartment. When you decide to act like a sensible woman instead of a skittish girl who's never been kissed, I'll come back to help you.''

Running into her room and slamming the door, Carissa thought that if Paul waited for that, he'd never come back. Why, after guarding her emotions for years, had she suddenly succumbed to the magnetism of Paul Spencer? Always before, she'd been so careful to keep men at an emotional distance, but for the past week, she'd been out of her element. Her usual contact with men was on a business basis and she often played the dominant role in those relationships. She'd never had a male friend, and because of his friendship, Paul had broken down her defenses.

She wanted to leave Yuletide, but she'd never run away from an obligation before. They had promised to take care of the children until after Christmas. If Paul didn't want to honor his promise, she'd manage alone, as she'd always had to do.

Paul untangled himself from the plastic bags and boxes, wondering if he'd injured himself. He'd felt a sharp pain when he'd landed on his left shoulder, and he sat up gingerly. If she'd injured him again, he wouldn't have the nerve to go to the local emergency room for treatment. He moved his arm back and forth, and found that it wasn't broken. Still angry, he went into the bedroom, picked up the clothes and personal articles he'd brought to the house and walked across the yard to his apartment.

Carissa Whitmore had been bad news for him from

the first minute he'd laid eyes on her. The last thing on his mind when he'd bought the mistletoe was that he'd kiss Carissa. Up until that minute, he'd thought of her as an interesting companion, and he'd admired her courage in taking on the responsibility of the children. He'd started to be wary when he'd learned she had a lot of money. That should have warned him to keep their relationship impersonal. But they'd had so much fun together while they were shopping and decorating the house that his defenses were down.

When Carissa had pushed him away, the humiliation he'd experienced when Jennifer jilted him had flashed before his eyes. Carissa was the only woman who had interested him since that time. To have her reject his advances had touched a raw nerve that he'd thought had healed a long time ago.

But regardless of what she'd done, Paul couldn't excuse himself for the vitriolic words he'd hurled at her. He'd never talked to anyone like that in his life. Not even to Jennifer, who'd hurt him so much. And he'd had the nerve to accuse Carissa of acting like a child! Well, he'd made a fool of himself, but if Carissa wouldn't make the first overture, it was all over between them.

But if he wasn't at the house, he wouldn't be able to help with the children. Serves her right, he thought. Hadn't Carissa brought this on herself by the way she'd reacted to a simple kiss? But was it a simple kiss? As best he could remember, his innocent, youthful intimacies with Jennifer hadn't given him the electric jolt he'd felt when his lips had touched Carissa's. Happiness such as he'd never known had made his spirits soar, and at that moment, even if he'd tried, he couldn't have resisted Carissa's appeal.

Well, the fox is in with the chickens now, he thought, recalling the old expression, and he didn't know what he could do about it.

When it was time to pick up the children, he drove into town as usual. It wasn't fair to Carissa to expect her to explain to the children why he wouldn't be staying at the house. Even a few days of tender care had made a difference in them. Uneasiness still lurked in the eyes of Alex and Lauren, but Julie was as carefree as if her future was certain. He would miss being at the house with them.

Paul was pleased to see that their children—and he wondered when he'd started thinking of them in that way—had made friends. Lauren and Alex seemed to have one or two companions when they left the school building, but Julie was always surrounded by several other children. She usually talked most of the time on the way home, telling of their school experiences.

When she'd finished, she asked, "What're we gonna have for supper, Uncle Paul?"

Now was the time to tell them. "I don't know. I'm staying in my apartment now, so Carissa will be doing the cooking."

Alex, who was sitting nearest the door holding Julie on his lap, glanced quickly at Paul.

"She's no cook. Said so herself," Alex said.

"I'm sure she'll have a good meal for you, but don't expect too much. She worked hard today decorating the house."

Julie's lips drew into a pout. "You said you'd watch cartoons with me tonight."

"I know I did, and I'm sorry. Some things came up, and I need to stay in my apartment."

"Uh-huh!" Alex said, and his expression became hard and resentful.

Paul stopped in front of the house and said, "I'll see you in the morning when I take you to school."

"I'm gonna stay with you," Julie said, a determined set to her little jaw.

"Forget it, Julie," Alex said, and he lifted her out of the truck.

When Carissa opened the door to greet them, she donned a smile.

"Oh," Lauren said as she looked at the decorations. "Pretty!"

Carissa hoped the Christmas decor would take their minds off Paul's absence.

"Let me help you out of your coats," she said with forced cheerfulness. "I bought some cookies at the deli yesterday, and you can have some with milk while we wait for dinner."

"I'm not hungry," Alex said, and stomped through the great room toward his room.

Lauren and Julie threw their coats on the couch and followed Carissa into the kitchen. They answered Carissa's questions in monosyllables, and as soon as they ate the two cookies and drank the small glasses of milk she allotted them, they picked up their coats and went upstairs.

Carissa sat at the table, her chin resting in her hand. What had Paul told the children that had upset them? Or had something happened at school?

Dinner, too, was a silent affair. As soon as they finished eating, Julie and Alex went into the great room, while Lauren stayed behind to help with the dishes.

Carissa soon became aware of an argument between Alex and Julie.

"I want to watch cartoons," Julie shouted.

"And I want to watch the hockey game," Alex said. "You're spoiled, Julie."

"Am not!"

"You are, too."

Julie tried to snatch the remote from Alex's grip. Carissa was surprised at Alex's reaction, for she'd noticed that both he and Lauren gave in to Julie. She knew it was time for her to intervene, but she didn't have the first clue about how to stop a quarrel between siblings.

"Thanks, Lauren, for helping," Carissa said, and with a sinking heart, she went into the great room.

"Julie, you've been watching cartoons for a half hour," she said. "It's Alex's turn to choose a show."

A belligerent light glittered in Julie's brown eyes. "No!"

"Then, go upstairs and watch the television in my room."

"No!" she shouted. "I'm gonna go and watch television with Uncle Paul. He'll let me watch my shows."

Julie started determinedly toward the back door. Carissa moved quickly and blocked the exit.

"No!" Carissa said. "Your place is here."

Julie started screaming, and kicked Carissa's leg savagely.

Carissa couldn't believe that this child, who'd been so sweet and outgoing for the past week, had turned into a little monster before her eyes.

Julie fell to the floor, kicking and screaming. Alex continued to watch television. Lauren stood behind the couch staring at her sister.

Rubbing her injured leg, Carissa said, "Well, what do we do? I told you I don't know anything about children."

"Nothing," Alex said. "She'll wear herself out after a while and cry herself to sleep."

"Sometimes Mama gave her time-out—made her go in a room by herself until she could behave," Lauren said.

"I wouldn't try that here," Alex advised. "When she has these fits, she sometimes throws things. Didn't matter at home, 'cause we didn't have nuthin': I don't want her to tear up this house."

Carissa certainly didn't want her to destroy any of Naomi's things, either, but she didn't know if she could stand the screaming much longer. Her nerves were already frayed from the emotional scene with Paul earlier in the day. He'd said he wouldn't come back until she needed him. She certainly needed him now—but she wouldn't call for him.

"Does she do this often?"

"Anytime she can't get her way," Lauren said.

"When our mom was so sick," Alex said, "we let her get by with a lot of stuff, so's not to worry Mom. But I'm tired of it."

Carissa limped to a chair and Lauren came to her.

"Did she hurt you bad?"

"Just a bruise, I think. I'll be all right."

Carissa made room in the chair for Lauren to sit beside her, but she held her hands over her ears. The child's piercing screams seemed to compound the pain in her head, which had been hurting for hours. She put her arm around Lauren, and the girl snuggled close to her. She knew these children needed a mother's love, but did she have any maternal love to give?

Julie's screams lessened gradually over the next hour and finally ceased. Lauren peered around the chair at her sister.

"She's asleep," Lauren whispered.

"Now what?" Carissa asked, feeling very foolish for having to ask for advice.

"Wait a while, and then we can take her to bed," Alex said.

After another half hour, Julie was still sound asleep. Lauren awakened her, and she docilely accepted Carissa's hand and went upstairs to bed.

"Is it all right if I stay up and watch television?" Alex asked.

"Keep the volume low and don't stay up too late," Carissa said. "I've had a hard day. I have to get some rest."

Lauren helped Julie undress and slip into her nightgown. "I'd better sleep with her," Lauren said.

"Surely that isn't necessary," Carissa said. There had only been two nights that Lauren had wet the bed, but she didn't want her to have an accident in Julie's bed. If these kids stayed much longer, she'd have to refurnish Naomi's house.

"I ought to, Miss Cara," Lauren responded, compassion in her voice. "She knows she's been bad, and she needs to know that we still love her, anyway."

Words of wisdom from such a small child, Carissa thought. She reached out and hugged Lauren tightly, for she needed love, too. Carissa swallowed a sob when Lauren leaned into her embrace.

"You're a good sister," Carissa said. "I'm going to bed, too, but call me if you need anything."

Carissa couldn't believe that such a tiny girl could have caused so much pain, but Julie had kicked her on the shinbone. She rubbed the affected area with some liniment she found in the medicine cabinet. She also took a couple of ibuprofen for the pain and swelling.

But she didn't go to sleep. All day long she'd avoided any thoughts about her altercation with Paul. She didn't blame him for his harsh words. She'd had them coming. Why hadn't she been wise enough to accept his kiss under the mistletoe as a friendly gesture and let it go at that? If she hadn't been so captivated by his words and leaned toward him, he wouldn't have done anything more. Why, oh why, had she let down her defenses to become enamored of Paul? For twenty years she'd built a wall between her and the male population—a wall high enough to keep all of them at a distance. When a man made romantic overtures, she froze him with a glance. Why hadn't she done that with Paul? The answer was simple—she hadn't cared about any of her other admirers. Paul was different.

She wanted him around her, so much so that she was afraid to admit it to herself.

Chapter Nine

Carissa finally drifted into a light sleep, only to be wakened by Lauren, who was shaking her shoulder.

"Miss Cara, come quick!" she said. "Julie's sick in the bed."

Fearing the worst, Carissa rushed into the other room. Julie was sitting up, gagging, and Carissa said, "Hurry. Into the bathroom."

"Too late," Lauren said, pointing at the comforter where Julie had already spewed the contents of her stomach.

Groaning, Carissa eased into a chair beside the bed to get her breath. The room smelled like a hospital, and nausea gripped Carissa. But she forced herself to deal with the situation.

"If you still feel sick, come to the bathroom with me," she said.

Julie took Carissa's hand and walked docilely to

the bathroom with Lauren trailing behind. Julie's gown was soiled.

"Could she have eaten something at school today that made her sick?" she asked Lauren.

"We had vegetable soup," Lauren said, "but she usually gets sick when she throws a temper fit."

"Please bring a clean nightgown, Lauren, while I wash her face and hands. Are you still feeling sick, Julie?"

"I don't think so."

"You'll have to sleep in Lauren's bed the rest of the night. I'll get some ginger ale from the refrigerator, and if you sip on that, it will settle your stomach."

When she went downstairs for the beverage, Alex was still watching television, and it was one o'clock in the morning.

"Julie's sick, huh?"

"Yes, and since you're still up, I'm going to take the soiled bedclothes to the basement and put them in the washer."

She cracked the upstairs window to clear the odor, tucked the girls into bed and covered them with a heavy blanket. Impulsively, she leaned down and kissed both girls' foreheads.

"Try to sleep now."

When she came up from the basement after putting the bed linens in the washer, she sat beside Alex on the couch. He muted the television volume.

"You should be in bed," she said.

"I'm too worried to sleep." When she didn't comment, he said, "You and Paul had a fight, didn't you."

"Do you think that's any of your concern?"

"Yes, it is. You both agreed to look after us, and I was starting to think things might work out for me and my sisters. We're gonna be dumped again."

"We didn't promise you anything permanent."

"I know, but I could hope, couldn't I? I can tell that you and Paul like each other, so I thought maybe you'd get married and adopt us."

Carissa put her hand over his clenched one. "Alex, Paul and I haven't known each other any longer than we've known you. We've lived into our forties without getting married—we're not apt to take such a step now. Marriage is a serious move for anyone, and especially for two people who are set in their ways. I'm sorry that you were expecting more than you'll get, but you knew this was a temporary situation from the first."

"I know that in a few weeks, it's going to be up to me to look out for my sisters again. But I trusted you to help us."

Trying to control her temper, Carissa crossed the floor and turned off the television. "Go to bed, Alex. I've had all I can handle today."

Sulkily, he obeyed her, and Carissa went upstairs wondering if Alex would try to run away again before morning. Without even changing into nightclothes she took off her shoes and slipped under the blankets. Emotionally and physically spent, at that moment, Carissa didn't care what happened.

Paul could tell by the woebegone expressions on the children's faces that all wasn't well. He drove slowly, hoping to find out what had happened the night before.

"Nice morning," he said, motioning to the snow-topped evergreen trees glistening in the morning sun. "Looks like nature is getting ready for Christmas, too."

No answer.

"How'd you like the decorations Carissa put up yesterday?"

"Nice," Lauren said.

After another period of silence, while Paul grew tense with apprehension, Julie said, "I was bad last night."

"You were worse than bad—you were a monster!" Alex said.

Julie's lower lip trembled. "I missed you, Uncle Paul."

"And when Miss Cara stood in front of the door to keep her from coming to your apartment," Lauren said, "she threw one of her fits and kicked Miss Cara on the leg."

"That wasn't a nice thing to do," Paul said, angry at himself because he'd deserted Carissa when she needed him.

"But it got worse," Alex said. "Julie screamed and carried on until she cried herself to sleep."

"Then she got sick and threw up in the bed," Lauren said. "We changed Julie's clothes. Then Miss Cara had to wash the sheets and things."

"And if Miss Cara puts us out, it will be Julie's fault," Lauren said.

"What makes you think she'll put you out?" Paul said.

"I wouldn't blame her if she did," Alex said.

"She looked awful sad while she was fixing our breakfast this morning," Julie said.

"Did you tell her you were sorry?"

Julie shook her head.

They had arrived at the school by then, and as the children left the truck, Paul said, "Don't worry about it today. You can apologize to Miss Cara tonight."

Paul parked the truck at the café and went inside to order his breakfast. In his anger, he'd told Carissa he wasn't returning until she asked him to. If she hadn't called for him the night before, when she was having so much trouble, it was obvious she wouldn't bend. Was it up to him to make the first move?

Paul had his pride, too, and it wasn't his nature to apologize for his actions. He knew he'd never forgiven Jennifer for her treatment of him. He hadn't railed at her the way he had at Carissa, but when Jennifer had written that she was breaking their engagement, asking for his understanding, he hadn't answered. He'd left Yuletide the next day and he'd neither seen nor heard from Jennifer since.

He sipped absentmindedly on his cup of coffee and stared into space. Through his stubbornness, was he going to allow his relationship with Carissa to fail? She was the only one who'd touched his heart in twenty years—in fact, he'd decided that he was incapable of loving again. He didn't think he was in love with Carissa yet, but given time, he believed he could learn to love her.

Pastor Erskine interrupted his reverie when he stopped by the booth where Paul sat and said that he wanted to have a committee meeting in the afternoon. Paul went back to his apartment and waited, hoping that Carissa would contact him and tell him about the episode of the night before. She didn't. He didn't see any sign of life at the house. Still not knowing what move to make, he waited until eleven o'clock before going over.

His heart pounding like a jackhammer, and wondering if Carissa would even speak to him, Paul stepped softly up on the deck. He lifted his hand to knock, and halted. Carissa was lying on the couch, on her back, one arm resting over her face in a defensive gesture. He watched for a few minutes, started to walk away, but then turned and knocked on the door. Carissa swung into a sitting position, rubbed her eyes and looked toward the door.

Would she turn him away?

She favored her right leg as she walked toward the door, and Paul realized that Julie's kick had hurt her.

She unlocked the door and turned back into the room. Presented with her back, Paul didn't know how to proceed. Somehow he perceived that apologies weren't necessary or perhaps even wanted.

"I saw Pastor Erskine in the café," he said. "He wants to have a meeting of the planning committee at one o'clock."

Carissa glanced at the clock. "Then, I'd better get ready." Without looking at Paul, she went upstairs.

He watched her rigid back with alarm. Her eyes had been icy and unresponsive. He wondered if he should call out his apologies to her. But he let her go without saying anything.

Carissa wondered if Paul intended for them to go together to the meeting, or if he'd return to his apartment and drive to town on his own. At that point, it really didn't matter to her. The episodes of the previous night had left her so depressed that she didn't care about anything. Not Paul. Not the Christmas celebrations. Not the children. Nothing.

When Carissa came down an hour later, feeling a little less exhausted after a shower, shampoo and a change of clothes, Paul was waiting in the kitchen.

"I'll have lunch ready in a few minutes," he said, as if no harsh words had ever passed between them.

Without answering, she sat at the table. He placed two grilled-cheese sandwiches and a plate of apple slices on the table. He'd brewed a pot of tea.

"I thought hot tea would go well. The bank sign registered zero this morning."

"I like a cup of hot tea on a frosty morning," Carissa replied.

They talked very little during lunch.

"The meeting will probably last until time for the kids to be out of school. If you want to take your SUV, we can bring them home."

When they left the house, she handed him her keys. "Will you drive, please?"

He took the keys, wondering why she wanted him to drive. Had Julie's kick injured her badly? Should she stop by the clinic? But Carissa had been making her own decisions for a long time. She didn't need a nursemaid, and in her present frame of mind, she'd be quick to tell him so. But Carissa didn't seem to be angry at him. She conveyed an "I just don't care" attitude, which alarmed him more than if she'd vented her anger on him.

The meeting lasted for two hours, and by the end, Carissa's head hurt so much that she could hardly concentrate. The lack of sleep and tension were taking their toll.

She wrote a check to pay for the light display that was already being erected on the lakeshore and gave it to Pastor Erskine. He said it would be operating a week before Christmas, and would stay lighted through New Year's Eve.

Two other women had volunteered to help Carissa with the costumes for the progressive nativity scene.

The pastor asked if she and Paul would play the roles of Mary and Joseph in the pageant, which would take place on the Sunday night before Christmas. They both agreed, but Carissa felt, rather than saw, the frequent glances Belva Townsend sent her way. As soon as the meeting adjourned, Belva drew Carissa aside and into a vacant room.

''I told you to contact me if you had any trouble,'' Belva said.

Eager to unburden herself to this knowledgeable woman, Carissa rubbed her head and said, ''I have a headache now, but my role as surrogate mother is really wearing me down.'' She told Belva about Lauren's bed-wetting habits, Julie's tantrum and the subsequent results, and Alex's hopes that she would keep them permanently. She omitted any mention of her relationship to Paul, and if the woman suspected that Carissa hadn't told her everything, she was wise enough not to mention it.

''Lauren's problem is a common one among children. The cause is usually a small bladder—it hasn't grown enough yet. Encourage her to go to the bathroom often, and, if you're awake in the middle of the night, see that she goes then. Pediatricians don't all agree with me, but I think the situation can be magnified by emotional distress. And the same thing probably caused Julie's tantrum. These children's mother died only a few weeks ago. They don't have a home, and they've been wandering around the state on their own. I noticed in school this morning that all three of them were not as exuberant as they'd been. Alex probably thinks you'll put them out because of the way Julie acted.''

''No matter what they do, I'll keep my promise to look after them until after Christmas,'' said Carissa. ''I tried to tell Alex last night that they need parents who know what they're doing. I'm ill-equipped by practice or temperament to take on a family of three. I'd be miserable, and they would be, too.''

''Paul promised to help,'' Belva reminded her.

''But he has to return to his job before the first of the year.''

''It *is* a dilemma,'' Belva agreed. ''They need love more than anything else—if we can only find someone to give it to them! I've put the situation on the prayer chain—our church family is praying for a solution. We'll have to find out who those children are and where they lived.''

''Julie has taken a distinct liking to Paul. He might be able to surprise the information out of her. But I don't suppose we should disrupt them any more until after Christmas.''

After the children were strapped into their seat belts for the drive to the house, in a quiet little voice, Julie said, ''I'm sorry for being so mean, Miss Cara.''

Carissa nodded and felt the pain increase. ''I know you are, Julie. Just forget about it. I'm sorry you were upset—perhaps I let my own problems override your needs. How did things go at school today?''

"Somebody stole some money," Lauren said, "and the pastor called us all into the auditorium and talked to us about stealing."

"Do they know who took the money?" Paul asked.

"He didn't say," Alex said.

When they arrived at the house, Julie tugged on Paul's hand and drew him inside. "I missed you last night," she said.

"It's good to be missed," he answered. "I'll make up for it by fixing what you like for supper. What do you want?"

"Spaghetti!" Julie said.

"No, pizza!" Lauren said.

Seeing Julie's pouting look, Paul knelt in front of her and helped her take off her snow boots.

"No more tantrums out of you, young lady. If you hadn't been so nasty, we'd have had spaghetti, but as it is, you'll have to wait until another time for your favorite. I guess I shouldn't have asked for suggestions, Lauren, because I don't have any pizza ingredients. We'll have pizza tomorrow night. Alex, you choose tonight's menu."

"I'd like to have chicken and mashed potatoes like Mom used to fix."

"Didn't we buy some chicken, Carissa?"

"Yes, it's in the freezer."

"Then I'll thaw it in the microwave and pop it in the oven to bake while I make the rest of dinner, which ought to be ready by six o'clock. Girls, you take your things upstairs, then come down and help me with dinner. Alex, you can bring in some wood from the deck so we can have a fire tonight. If you have homework, we can take care of it after dinner.''

When all of the children denied having assignments, Paul looked keenly at Carissa. ''You'll probably find some headache medicine in Naomi's medicine cabinet. Close your door, and I'll keep the kids quiet while you take a rest.''

Tears misted her eyes, and she went upstairs without answering. Paul had evidently come back to stay, and she hadn't had to ask him to.

She didn't take any medication, but she did stretch out in the large recliner chair in the bedroom. She pulled a hand-crocheted afghan over her shoulders and dozed contentedly. She glanced at her watch occasionally, and at six o'clock, she went downstairs.

The aroma of food, mixed with a smell of burning wood, filled the house. She paused on the bottom step. All the decorations seemed enhanced by the gently-burning fire, making the great room the most homelike place Carissa had ever seen.

''We were going to let you sleep a little longer before we called you,'' Lauren said.

''I didn't sleep, but I rested some. Dinner smells great,'' she said.

''All of us helped,'' Alex said.

''Then I suppose I'll have to take care of the dishes—since I didn't help cook.''

The children were cheerful again—so different

from the way they'd been the previous night. As they ate together and then sat on the floor around the fireplace to pop corn the old-fashioned way, they seemed like a family. Paul and Carissa exchanged questioning glances, but Carissa could see no further than the present. She was happy they could provide some security for the children for a few weeks, but she couldn't conceive of this being a permanent arrangement.

The warmth of the fire and the cessation of her headache made Carissa very sleepy, and after watching her yawn every few minutes, Paul said, "I don't think anyone got much sleep last night. Let's go to bed early tonight."

"Girls, head upstairs and get ready for bed. I'll be up in a minute," Carissa said. Remembering Belva's observation that the children needed love more than anything else, she went to Alex and put her arm around his waist, giving him a slight squeeze. "Thanks for helping with your sisters. I'm sure your mother would be proud of you."

He hung his head and moved out of Carissa's embrace. "I don't think she would be," he said, and went to his room.

Carissa lifted troubled eyes to Paul. She'd thought her gesture would encourage Alex, but apparently it hadn't. Whenever she thought she was learning how to treat the children, she ran into a wall.

"The teen years are difficult ones," Paul said. "You're doing okay."

She shook her head. "I don't know."

When she turned away, Paul said, "Are we going to keep pretending nothing has happened? Or are we going to talk?"

"We'll talk, but not when there are three pairs of interested ears in the house. Besides, I'm too weary to talk tonight."

Halfway up the stairs, Carissa turned to find Paul watching her. He captured her eyes with his, and his look of tenderness made her heart ache. She'd told him they would have to talk tomorrow. But how could she explain her fondness for him, while at the same time revealing the reason she'd reacted so strangely to his caresses? Would the hang-ups she'd carried from youth into maturity ruin her friendship with Paul?

"Goodnight, Carissa," he said softly. "Sleep well."

When she tried to answer, her voice faltered, but before she made a hasty retreat to her bedroom, she threw him a kiss.

Chapter Ten

After Paul left to take the children to school, Carissa cleared the kitchen table and started making sketches for the costumes needed for the nativity scenes. She had an afternoon appointment at the church with the other two women who were helping with the costumes. Belva had said there was a fabric shop in town where they could buy the necessary materials at a discount. They would need twenty-five garments, and it would involve a lot of sewing. Luckily, she had brought her favorite portable machine with her.

She hadn't gotten far with her designing when Paul returned. She heard his truck in the driveway, and she wondered if he would go to the apartment. If he didn't, the long-overdue talk must take place.

"Am I interrupting?" Paul said as he entered the

kitchen, bringing the outdoor fragrance of wintertime with him.

Carissa's hands wrapped tightly around her pencil. "I'm making sketches of the costumes we need for the pageant."

"I thought we could talk now, but if you're too busy..." His voice trailed off.

"Let me finish the lines of this shepherd's robe so I won't forget what's in my mind. I'll join you in the great room in a few minutes."

Even as she finished the sketch, Carissa's heartbeat accelerated and she had trouble focusing on what she was doing. The hour of reckoning had come—the time when she knew that, for her continued happiness, she must talk about things that would be difficult to reveal.

She poured two glasses of apple juice, and handed one to Paul as she entered the great room. He sat on the couch, and she chose a chair directly opposite him. She needed to look him in the eye while they talked.

"I want to apologize for what happened," Paul said. "I can't say I'm sorry I kissed you, because I enjoyed it, but I am sorry I did it when you didn't want me to."

Carissa waved aside his apologies. "I'm not mad at you—I'm mad at myself. I accept the blame. There's no excuse for my behavior. It was only a brotherly kiss at first, but my reaction invited more."

Paul wondered at the look of humiliation in Carissa's eyes.

"Why does my touch disturb you?"

She shook her head. "This isn't easy for me to say. You accused me of acting like a girl who'd never been kissed. And that's true. I hadn't been kissed before."

Paul stared at her in disbelief. "What's the matter with the men you've met through the years?" he asked, a tinge of wonder in his voice. "You're a vivacious, charming woman."

Her heart hammered foolishly at his words, but she made an effort to speak calmly. "I made up my mind a long time ago that I wanted to avoid a close relationship with any man."

She swallowed hard, gripped the sides of the chair and closed her eyes for a moment.

Paul was aware that this revelation was hard for Carissa, and he wondered if he should tell her that she didn't have to explain. He didn't speak, however, for he sensed that Carissa needed to unburden herself of the frustration that had blighted her emotional life.

She opened her eyes. "I'm an illegitimate child," Carissa started, in a voice that was barely more than a whisper. "My mother never married, and she had lots of male companions, so I have no idea who my father is. My mother died when I was a child, before I knew what kind of person she was. After her death, it didn't take long for the kids to let me know that my mother had been a prostitute."

After a few minutes of silence, she glanced at Paul. His face revealed consternation at what she'd told him.

"Like me any less than you did?" she asked with a wry smile.

"Of course not! You aren't accountable for what your mother did."

"You'd have thought I was if you'd lived through my childhood in a small town. I had a few friends, but they were mostly older people in our church. But I looked very much like my mother, and I heard more than once 'Like mother, like daughter.' By the time I reached my teen years, everyone was expecting me to turn out just like her. I couldn't do anything about looking like her, but I made up my mind that I wouldn't be promiscuous, too. The only way I knew to avoid that was to stay away from the opposite sex. I refrained from any casual friendships with men, fearing they might develop into something more. I was determined that I'd never have children who would be ashamed of me as I am of my mother."

"I'm sorry to hear about your parentage and the difficult childhood, but..." He paused, wondering how to continue. "But why did you push me away? I had nothing to do with that."

Sadness had darkened her blue eyes while she'd unloaded the trauma of her past, and she couldn't meet his gaze now. She stood and walked to the window that looked out upon the wooded mountain behind the chalet.

"Because I *wanted* you to kiss me, and I didn't want you to stop. When I realized that I'd let my emotions overrule my principles, I was scared. Terrified of how I was feeling—strange, uncomfortable feelings I'd never experienced before."

She felt Paul's presence behind her, and she clenched her fists, praying he wouldn't touch her again. How would she react if he did?

He didn't touch her, but his voice was tender when he said, "I know it wasn't easy for you to reveal this, and I'm honored that you'd tell me. But you're not a vulnerable girl anymore. And there's nothing wrong with the emotions you experienced. You're a mature woman who won't submit to the shortcomings of your mother. Come and sit down."

Noting the weary droop of Carissa's shoulders, Paul's arms ached to embrace her. He almost believed that Carissa wanted him to take her into his arms, but he'd have to be more sure of that to try again. She turned away, and he hoped she would sit beside him on the couch, but when she didn't, he knew he must be cautious in what he did and said.

"To be honest," Paul said, "I wasn't too happy with my reactions to our kiss, either."

She lifted her head quickly, and her expressive eyes revealed a hint of sadness. Had he used the wrong words?

"Since you've been so honest with me, I think it's only fair to tell you why I've never married. During my last two years in high school, I dated a local girl,

Jennifer Pruett. We were in love. We planned to be married after graduation and attend college to-gether.''

Carissa watched the play of emotions on his face. Pain and anger glittered in his dark eyes.

''The summer after our graduation, Jennifer went to visit her aunt in New York City, where she met a man she wanted more than she wanted me. An older man who could give her a lot more than I could. He was wealthy, and when she compared all he had to the four years we'd have to spend in college living from hand to mouth, she chose riches instead of me. She sent me a 'Dear John' letter, which I didn't an-swer. I left Yuletide and I haven't seen Jennifer since. Her mother still lives in town, but I've been fortunate enough not to encounter Jennifer during the few visits I've made here.''

''Where is she now?''

''Last I heard she'd divorced her husband, but was still living in the New York City area. I'm not sure I've ever forgiven her, but the way she treated me convinced me that I was better off staying a bachelor. I didn't want to get hurt again. So when I kissed you, I wasn't happy about it. I thought I'd put those emo-tions out of my life. Then, when you pushed me away, I experienced the same sense of rejection that I'd had after Jennifer jilted me.''

''I'm sorry I made you remember.''

''Maybe it's just as well for me to remember. As long as the past festers in my heart, I'm not the kind of person God wants me to be. And the longer we work toward bringing Christmas to Yuletide, the more it makes me realize that I've not honored God by the way I've lived. My only concern has been Paul Spencer, and no one else.''

''I understand what you mean,'' she said. ''Helping with the celebration and looking after our children has caused me to look at my own spiritual needs.''

''So now that we know and understand each other's hang-ups, where do we go from here? Seems to me we've been getting along pretty well the past three weeks, so if you're willing, let's forget our past problems and concentrate on finding Christmas—the way we'd both planned. I believe we'll find it by caring for the children and bringing Christmas to Yuletide.''

He reached out a hand to her. After only slight hesitation, Carissa took it, and he helped her to her feet.

''Of course I'm willing. I haven't had many close friends, and I've enjoyed our few days together. And the children will be relieved, too. They detected the tension between us. Alex even asked if we'd had a fight, and said he supposed he'd have to start looking out for his family again.''

''And speaking of that, I'm concerned about something else. I wonder if Alex took the money that disappeared from school. Maybe he's accumulating some money so they can run away again.''

"Oh, no! I've coped with Lauren's bed-wetting problem and Julie's tantrums. I won't overlook stealing."

"You won't have to. I've already set a trap for Alex. I had an old billfold in the apartment. I put a few dollars in it and placed it on a shelf beside the washer and dryer. We'll see what happens. I suspect that Alex was stealing, even before his mother died, to help with the family's upkeep."

"Stealing was one offense I wouldn't tolerate in my company," Carissa said grimly, her blue eyes darkening. "Evidence of theft meant automatic dismissal. And to think I've taken in a child who may steal."

"We don't know that yet," Paul said. "But I wanted you to know my suspicions so you'd watch your purse."

"Yes, I will. Thanks, Paul, for listening to me. It's been too convenient through the years for me to ignore things that bothered me. But now...I have to go back to my work. The sketches have to be finished before this afternoon. I've promised to cut out the patterns, and the other two ladies will do most of the sewing."

"I'm going out on the lake now to try some fishing. That will give you some peace and quiet to work. I'll drive into town with you this afternoon and help with the rest of the street decorations."

A half hour later, Carissa watched through the window as Paul, heavily clothed, walked toward the lake. His presence did disturb her peace of mind, so it was just as well that he had left the house for a short time. Still, she couldn't tear her gaze from his long athletic stride and the proud set of his head. Carissa knew that her feelings for him were intensifying to a point of no return.

Paul returned, empty-handed, at eleven o'clock, but he'd had a good morning. The cold air had added a ruddy hue to his dark skin, and contentment gleamed in his eyes.

"It's a good day for skating," he said. "Maybe we can rent some skates and take the kids out on the ice."

Carissa had finished her sketches and had a light lunch ready, which they sat down to. The doorbell rang, however, before they finished eating.

They'd had no visitors other than Justin and Belva, so Carissa was surprised to answer and find a woman at the door.

Carissa took in the visitor's appearance quickly. Tall and willowy, with black hair and glowing green eyes, this woman would be a perfect model for Cara's Fashions. Her leather jacket was open, and, coincidentally, her sweater was one of Carissa's creations.

"Hello," the woman said. "I'm looking for Paul Spencer. I understand he's living here."

"Well, yes," Carissa said slowly as she opened

the door. "Come in—Paul," she called, "you have company."

He sauntered into the great room and glanced at the visitor, and his face whitened. His eyes widened in astonishment.

The woman went toward him with outstretched hand, and when Paul ignored her hand, she leaned forward and kissed him lightly on the lips. He moved away, and she laughed.

"That's not the way you reacted the last time I kissed you," she said. "I thought some things would never change."

Turning as if she'd suddenly remembered Carissa's presence, the woman said, "Maybe I'm out of line." Nodding toward Carissa, she said, "I hadn't heard that you were married."

His astonishment soon turned to annoyance, and in a curt voice Paul said, "I'm not married. This is my friend, Carissa Whitmore." And with a meaningful glance toward Carissa, who had an unfathomable expression in her eyes, he continued, "Carissa Whitmore, meet Jennifer…Pruett. I don't remember your married name."

Jennifer smiled. "It's Colton. Jennifer Colton. It seems you've forgotten a lot of things about me, while I've never forgotten *anything* about you." She slid her fingertips across his left cheek in a provocative gesture before walking to the couch and sitting down without an invitation.

''If you'll excuse me,'' Carissa said, ''I have some work to finish.''

Uneasy, Paul wondered what Jennifer was up to now. How he wished she'd stayed out of his life!

He watched Carissa climb the steps, wanting her to stay but knowing he shouldn't ask it of her. If Jennifer wanted to talk to him, he might as well get it over with. As he waited for Jennifer to speak, he compared the present Jennifer with the one he'd loved. Had she always had that determined thrust to her jaw and that hardness in her eyes? Or had the eyes of love and youth blinded him to her true character?

''I've wanted to see you since we parted,'' Jennifer said, ''but apparently you haven't spent much time in Yuletide.''

''Only a few times to visit Naomi. Yuletide held nothing else of interest to me.''

''I came to visit Mother for a few days, intending to take her home with me for Christmas. Now that I find you're here, I may just spend Christmas in Yuletide.'' She nodded her head toward the upstairs. ''Or do your interests...lie in that direction?''

Paul was determined that Jennifer wouldn't learn how much she'd hurt him, and he forced himself to speak in a composed voice. ''Carissa and I met about three weeks ago. She and Naomi have traded houses for a few months. Your mother may have told you that three runaway kids have come to Yuletide. Carissa and I are looking after them until further arrangements can be made.''

''How cozy!'' Jennifer exclaimed.

When Paul remained silent, Jennifer stood and said, ''Well, you won't be baby-sitting all the time. Perhaps we can have dinner some evening.''

He followed her to the door. ''Carissa and I are helping with the town's celebration, so we're very busy.''

''Oh, well, I'll see you around somewhere,'' Jennifer said breezily as she strolled down the sidewalk, jaunty and self-assured.

Chapter Eleven

Carissa sat in the window seat and leaned her head on her knees. Jennifer Colton's physique was the kind Carissa had always dreamed of having. Carissa had resented the fragile features and the light coloring she'd inherited from her mother. As a child, she'd often fantasized about being a tall, slender brunette, and she'd created Cara's Fashions for that type of woman. Jennifer could easily have been one of the cover girls that appeared on her company's brochures.

The woman's arrival today had ruined the friendship that she'd started to enjoy with Paul, ruined whatever relationship might have developed between them. Anyone could tell from the predatory look in Jennifer's eyes that she intended to go after Paul again, as she'd done in her youth. And what were Paul's feelings toward her? He had said he'd loved her once. Had that love disappeared when Jennifer jilted him and married another man? Carissa doubted it, thinking that might be the reason Paul hadn't been interested in any other women.

Not for the first time, Carissa wished she'd never made this move to Yuletide. She'd been getting along very well on her own, but in just a few days, she'd become dependent on Paul's companionship for her emotional needs. It would be doubly hard when she had to go alone again.

She heard a car leave the driveway and assumed Jennifer was leaving. Carissa dreaded to find out Paul's reaction to seeing his former girlfriend. Her stomach churned with anxiety when she heard his soft tread on the steps. He tapped lightly on the half-closed door. She straightened on the window seat, grateful that in spite of her sadness, she was dry-eyed.

"Come in," she said.

Paul walked in, and Carissa's suspicion that he was pleased that Jennifer had reentered his life was immediately dispelled.

He said bitterly, "I don't know why she had to show up at this particular time. How she has the nerve to face me I can't imagine."

So his reaction to seeing her again was anger, Carissa thought. But sometimes anger covered other emotions. He could be angry and still love Jennifer.

Paul paced for a few minutes. "After I got over the blow to my self-esteem when she broke our engagement, I was able to realize that her emotions weren't as deeply involved as mine had been. She wanted a husband, and Yuletide didn't offer a large selection. I suppose I was the best one she could find here. When she visited the big city, she found men that suited her more.''

He sat on the edge of the bed.

''Maybe she's back in your life for a reason,'' Carissa said. ''When I talked to you about my anger and frustration with my mother, it relieved me of a burden I've carried for years. Maybe you haven't resolved your anger, and this will give you an opportunity to do so. Harboring such sentiments for years isn't easy. I know.''

Paul knew one reason he was so angry: for the first time since his attachment to Jennifer, he'd become deeply interested in another woman. Carissa had been on his mind constantly since he'd met her, and it was pleasant to contemplate the rest of the month with her. When they had to part on the first of January, he didn't know what commitments he might want to make.

Now he had the feeling that Jennifer hoped to rekindle their romance. Surely he had enough willpower not to succumb to her charms, which had fascinated him when he was a teenager. But he remembered that Jennifer could be very persuasive and was unsure of how he'd react.

''Maybe she's had time to realize what she gave up when she let you go.''

"I'm not that much of a catch," he said. "Not with all the possibilities in the Big Apple."

Knowing how she was drawn to him herself, Carissa wasn't so sure. Obviously Jennifer had everything a woman could desire. Wealth, charm, good looks—perhaps everything except the devoted love of a man. If love had eluded her, then Jennifer might look for it in Paul.

Carissa vowed to put aside thoughts of a possible reconciliation between Jennifer and Paul as she helped Yuletide prepare to resurrect the Christmas spirit.

The night that the display of lights around the lake was turned on, Paul and Carissa went with the children to the opening celebration, when the mayor threw the switch to illuminate the Christmas Fantasy show.

The five of them walked the mile-long route to view the wonderland of lights. The largest display represented a tall ice castle. Others represented the joy of the holiday season—an ice-skating family, a group of carolers standing beside a lamppost, a horse-drawn buggy, and many animated toys.

The real meaning of Christmas was commemorated in scenes depicting the birth of Christ—three Wise Men approaching on camels; angels announcing the birth of Jesus to shepherds watching a flock of sheep; and the nativity scene with Mary, Joseph and the baby in the stable surrounded by several farm animals.

Paul had prepared logs for a fire before they left, and when they returned to the house, while Carissa prepared hot chocolate, he and the children popped corn in the fireplace.

It occurred to Carissa that it seemed unnatural that the children seldom talked about their home life. Their mother had been dead only a short time. Surely they missed her. By refusing to voice their sorrow, were they pretending they were happy?

But tonight, instead of sitting with the others around the fire, Lauren huddled in a deep chair, and Carissa pondered if this sensitive child was remembering the past.

"Don't you want to sit closer to the fire, Lauren?" Carissa asked, touching her hand. "You feel cold."

"The last time I touched Mommy, she was awful cold," Lauren whispered, and her eyes filled with tears.

Carissa moved to the chair and sat beside the child.

Tears brimming in her eyes, Lauren asked, "Is she still cold? They buried her in the ground."

Carissa lifted terrified eyes toward Paul. She didn't know how to deal with Lauren's hurt.

Julie rushed over to pat Lauren on the head, and Alex said, "I told you people don't get cold in heaven."

"Is that true, Miss Cara?" Julie asked.

Praying for guidance, Carissa tried to remember

the words her grandmother had used to console her when she lost her mother.

"When your mother died, she left her earthly body behind. She has a new, spiritual body, and I'm sure she isn't cold." Carissa's mouth seemed parched, and she looked to Paul for help.

"From what you've told us," he said, "your mother had been very sick for a long time. Maybe God took her to be with Him so she wouldn't hurt anymore. Try to think of your mother being in a place where she's happy."

"She didn't have happiness here on earth," Alex said bitterly. "I miss her, but I was glad when she died because she wouldn't be sick anymore."

"That's the way to look at it, Alex," Paul said. "Why don't you remember the good times you had with your mother—that's a good way to forget her illness."

"We've got a picture of all of us before Mama got sick, but Alex won't let us look at it," Lauren said.

Carissa turned on Alex. "Why not?"

"Because they both start crying, and I can't stand it."

"They need to cry," Paul said, "and so do you. You're only a boy, even if you've had a man's burden put on you. Where is the picture?"

"With my things."

"Go and get it. I'd like to see your mother's picture," Carissa said gently.

Reluctantly, Alex went into his room and came back with a large photo taken by a professional photographer. He handed the picture to Lauren, and Julie hung over her shoulder to look.

"See, that's me," she said, pointing to a curly-headed toddler on the lap of a sad-faced but beautiful woman sitting in the center of the photo. Lauren and Alex stood on either side of the woman. All three children had pleasant, carefree expressions on their faces, so apparently their home life hadn't been too bad before their mother became ill.

"We couldn't afford anything but the free copy," Alex said.

"It's a very nice picture, and the next time we go to Saratoga Springs, we'll take this picture and get a copy for each of you," Carissa said. "Your mother was very pretty. And I know how much you miss her— I was about Julie's age when my mother died."

"Is there a tombstone on your mother's grave?" Alex asked, his face troubled.

"Yes. Not a big one, but my grandmother marked the grave."

"There's none on Mom's, except the little metal marker the undertaker put on it."

Carissa was tempted to tell him that she'd buy a marker for the grave, but she'd have to know where the cemetery was. That might be a sly way to dig into their past, but tonight wasn't the time to be devious. The children needed to be loved.

"Let's sing some Christmas carols," she suggested. "While we sing, think about the good times you had with your mother. Instead of being bitter about the past, all of us should think about positive things," she added with a pointed look at Paul.

Smiling, he lifted his hand in a salute to show that he'd gotten her meaning and swung into the opening lyrics of "Joy to the World."

The next day when Jennifer Colton attended the committee meeting, however, Carissa was hard put to follow her own advice.

"I'm so proud of my hometown for resurrecting Christmas," Jennifer said as soon as the pastor started the meeting.

Even Carissa with her suspicions about Jennifer couldn't tell if the woman was being honest. "But there's one more thing needed to make this celebration like the ones we used to have. We need to have a skating party." Jennifer looked with glowing eyes at some of the older people in the room, whom she apparently knew.

Paul's heart plummeted, and he turned a despairing glance in Carissa's direction.

"Do you remember the great times we used to have?" Jennifer asked. "We had competitions and gave prizes for the best acts. If you're interested in trying this again, I'll organize it and take care of all the expenses."

Paul thought Jennifer must have learned about

Carissa's generous contribution for the light display. As he remembered, Jennifer always wanted to outdo everyone else.

When the committee chairman put the idea to a vote, only Paul dissented. Regardless of the way Jennifer's presence had disturbed her, Carissa knew she couldn't let personal bias rule decisions that would be good for the town, so she voted in favor of the skating party.

Carissa didn't think her emotional roller coaster could plunge any lower, but it did when, with a hearty laugh, Belva asked, "You and Paul going to perform like you used to?"

"I hadn't thought of that—" Jennifer said.

Carissa believed she was lying, that this was another ploy to get her hooks in Paul.

"That would be great. What about it, Paul?" Jennifer asked.

Paul was convinced that Jennifer had planned this whole thing with the goal of forcing him back into a relationship with her. In the days of their courtship, Paul had overlooked some of her obvious faults. Disillusioned now, he remembered character traits that hadn't been endearing. The boys had liked Jennifer, but she hadn't cultivated the friendship of girls.

"I haven't had many opportunities to skate lately," Paul said, "so I'm out of practice. Sorry."

"I figure skating is like riding a bicycle," Belva said. "Once you learn how, you never forget."

"That's true," Jennifer said excitedly. "And I've

kept up with skating. It won't take long for me to teach you any techniques you've forgotten.''

Paul shook his head. ''And I weigh about fifty pounds more than I did when I was in high school. I'm not very graceful anymore, so it wouldn't be much of a performance.''

''But you're still in good shape,'' Jennifer said, unashamedly admiring his solid shoulders and trim waist. She reached out and patted Paul's forearm. ''It'll be fun.'' With glowing eyes, she turned to the pastor's secretary. ''Put us down for a performance. I'll come to your office in the morning to make plans about getting others enrolled in the competition.''

Paul felt like a drowning man searching for a life preserver. ''I don't know that I'll participate,'' he said. ''I'll think about it and let you know in a day or two.''

''But time is running out. We'll have to move quickly,'' Pastor Erskine said.

''I'll think about it and let you know in a day or two,'' Paul repeated evenly, and he looked at Jennifer.

''If you make an announcement indicating that we'll be skating before I agree to it, you'll skate alone.''

An angry look crossed Jennifer's face, but she said with a strained laugh, ''All right! All right! But decide as soon as possible.''

''Have you had another fight?'' Alex said as they were driving home.

Paul turned furiously toward the back seat, but Carissa nudged him in the side.

"Paul and I haven't had the *first* fight, so how could we have *another* one? Just because you're living with us doesn't give you the right to involve yourself in our personal affairs. But I will tell you that Paul has been upset by something that has nothing to do with you or your sisters. So stop being nosy!"

"Yes, ma'am," he said. "Sorry."

As they drove the rest of the way in silence, Carissa considered the aunts and uncles who'd not wanted to take all three of these children. She could understand why, because all three of them had distinct personalities. She thought she could deal well enough with any one of the three, but she didn't think she could cope with all three. Natural parents became accustomed to their children's differences gradually, but to suddenly take on the responsibility of caring for three children was daunting. Short of adopting these children, what else could she do for them?

After Paul helped with the dishes, he said, "I'm going out for a walk."

"I want to go with you, Uncle Paul," Julie said, and headed for the closet to get her coat.

"Not tonight, Julie," he said. "I have some thinking to do."

Julie stamped her feet. "I want to go."

He knelt beside her. "Julie, you *are not* going with

me. Sit with your family and watch television for a while and then get ready for bed.''

''Please!'' Her chin quivered, and Paul wasn't unaffected by her gesture. It had been balm to his heart that this little girl adored him so much, but he knew it wasn't good to give in to the child's demands. Besides, he had to be alone tonight.

''No,'' he said firmly. ''Give me a hug and then behave yourself.''

Sniffling, Julie hugged his neck, and Carissa wondered if she'd throw a tantrum as soon as Paul was out of the house.

Looking at Carissa, a resigned expression on his face, he said, ''I don't know when I'll be back, so don't wait up for me. I have a key.''

Julie's eyes followed Paul until he was out of sight. Still sniffling, she sat on the floor and watched the program Alex had chosen.

Carissa was sympathetic to Julie's feelings. She would have liked to accompany Paul, too. The uneasy nagging in the back of her mind refused to be silenced. Paul needed some time to decide if he still wanted Jennifer. Carissa dreaded the decision he might make during his walk.

Chapter Twelve

Paul avoided the lakefront, where he would encounter other people looking at the Christmas Fantasy lights. He took a flashlight from the glove compartment of his truck and headed up the mountain. He soon accessed a trail made by loggers several years ago, which was kept in usable condition for safety purposes during the forest-fire season.

The days he'd spent with Carissa and the children had been the most satisfying time he'd known in years. After the first dreadful months following his breakup with Jennifer, he'd been content with his nomadic life. But recently, he'd started thinking about settling down in one place, wondering if he was too old to become a family man. Many men he knew had married in their forties, and had fathered children.

So why, when his thoughts were veering in that

direction, had Jennifer come back into his life? He had no doubt that he'd loved Jennifer at one time, but he believed it was over. When she'd shown up yesterday, he hadn't experienced any of the pleasure or excitement she had once caused. Didn't that indicate that he was indifferent to what she said or did?

After Jennifer ditched him, Paul had pushed all memories of their painful relationship into the background. But today, little by little, as he walked, Paul dredged from the depths of his memory the two years he and Jennifer had dated.

Jennifer's family had moved to Yuletide when she was sixteen. She'd been the most beautiful girl in their school, and he was flattered when she chose him. He wondered now if he'd been chosen not because she loved him, but because he was the most eligible guy in school. Yuletide was a small place, and Paul had been captain of the football team and had played on all the other sports teams. He was also the only man in town who excelled at skating. Had she loved him or had she chosen him only because he fitted her needs at the time?

In retrospect, he realized that even as a teenager, Jennifer had been manipulative. He remembered with sorrow one time when his parents had planned for all of them to attend a family reunion in Vermont. The date conflicted with the time that Jennifer's family was going to the beach. He still didn't know how it happened, but Paul ended up going to the beach with the Pruetts.

He'd felt lousy for disappointing his parents, who had gone to the reunion with Naomi and her husband. He'd promised, ''The next time I'll go with you,'' but his father died before the next reunion.

He'd apparently been putty in Jennifer's hands, for he remembered countless other times that he'd set aside his plans because she'd wanted him to. He'd tell himself that he wouldn't do it, but the next thing he knew, Jennifer got her way.

Paul's mother hadn't liked Jennifer, and now he could understand why. His mother had told him when they announced their engagement that he was making a mistake—that Jennifer would ruin his life.

Jennifer hadn't been pleased with his plans to be an engineer. She'd wanted them to become professional skaters. He liked to skate, but he wasn't thrilled with the intense competition and the rigid life of a professional. After Jennifer broke their engagement, he'd moved to California, finished his engineering degree and started his overseas work. He'd blocked Jennifer out of his mind and life. But now she was back. He didn't want her—but was he strong enough to withstand her charm and seductive ways if he saw her every day? She'd wrapped him around her finger once…so should he avoid her now? Or was it better to skate with her and prove to her and *himself,* once and for all, that she had no hold on him?

And what would Carissa think about it? After yesterday—when he and Carissa had unburdened their past hang-ups and explanations about why they'd never married—his feelings for her had intensified, as if the future held something more for them than they realized.

He didn't want anything to jeopardize their relationship, if that was what God wanted for them. If he skated with Jennifer, he might lose an opportunity to explore a future with Carissa. On the other hand, he didn't want to go through life wondering if Jennifer had any hold on him.

Breathless, he reached a clearing on the top of the mountain, affording a view of Yuletide and the lake. He easily picked out Naomi's house. What were Carissa and the children doing now? As he watched, the lights faded on the first floor, and he knew they'd gone to bed. When the deck light came on, he realized that Carissa had left a light on for him. How much would Carissa care if he and Jennifer were reconciled?

He sat on the boulder until the crisp night air chilled his body. He knew what he had to do—but was he man enough to do it? He'd lived for years in a man's world, one that had given him very little experience in dealing with inner emotions and needs of the heart. He now faced a new situation—his emotions in conflict between two women. One whom he'd once loved, and another whom he believed he *could* love, given time and opportunity.

He had already committed to being Joseph in the living nativity and Carissa would be Mary. They would be together often, planning and practicing for their roles. And if he accepted Jennifer's challenge, and he believed that was what it was, he'd be with her every day, too. Which woman would win his heart?

He considered the five-year age difference between Carissa and him. He had trouble believing that Carissa was forty-five, because she had a vulnerable, untouched air that prompted him to protect her. He believed he could help her forget her unfortunate past—but he didn't have much time. In two weeks, he had to return to work in Europe.

Discouraged, and still undecided about what to do about Jennifer, Paul strode quickly down the mountain trail. The waning moon provided some light, and the glow on the deck served as a beacon to guide him. Or was Carissa the lodestar that lighted his way?

Carissa heard the wind blowing around the house, and she shivered under her warm blanket. The illuminated clock face indicated it was past midnight. Paul had been gone for more than three hours, and she wondered if he was all right. She'd dozed a little, but for the most part she'd stayed awake, worrying that Paul would go back to Jennifer.

She indulged in several minutes of self-pity, wishing she had Jennifer's beauty. She compared her small body and insignificant features to the perfection of Jennifer's appearance. If it came to a choice between her and Jennifer, she wouldn't blame Paul if he chose Jennifer. And Jennifer was closer to Paul's age. Being five years his senior didn't make her eligible for a romantic relationship with him.

Carissa didn't like Jennifer's flamboyant personality, but she attributed that to jealousy. She disliked pettiness in anyone, and she was disgusted that she'd stoop so low, even in her thoughts.

Remembering Belva's admonition that Lauren should take frequent trips to the bathroom, Carissa went to the other bedroom and awakened the child to go. Carissa hadn't put on a robe, so she was colder than ever when she got back to her bed. She turned the blanket heat up a couple of notches, hoping she would go to sleep, but she was still awake when she heard Paul enter the house an hour later. She would have liked to talk to him.... No, Paul would have to initiate any conversation about his relationship with Jennifer.

"Brr!" Paul greeted her when she entered the kitchen the next morning. He pointed to a dual thermometer on the wall. The outside temperature hovered slightly above zero.

"No wonder I felt cold last night," Carissa said.

"The furnace is on a timer that reduces the temperature a few degrees at night. Naomi and her husband didn't like to sleep in a warm house."

"I'm worried about the children's clothing," she said, trying to talk of mundane matters to keep her mind off Paul and Jennifer. "The things they got at the church are all right, but they need heavier footwear. I'll pick them up after school and take them shopping. I noticed a department store in Yuletide that should have what they need."

"I'll share the expense with you, Carissa. Remember, this a joint venture."

"Then you might as well go along with us as we shop. I don't know anything about buying boots for kids."

Their routine was well established. Paul prepared breakfast for everyone, and she took care of the dishes while he drove the children to school. Carissa was vacuuming when Paul returned. When she finished, he put the vacuum cleaner in the broom closet, then stood by the fireplace, his arm resting on the mantel.

"Well, Jennifer really wrecked my plans for a laid-back Christmas celebration," he said. "She wasn't content to be a disruptive element in my life twenty years ago—she had to come back now."

"I assumed you took the walk to decide what to do. I've had no experience along this line, but I suppose once you love someone, the emotion is always there."

He looked at her quickly. "I'm not in love with Jennifer now, if that's what you're suggesting."

Carissa's heart exploded with a little leap of gladness. "Then why should her return to Yuletide disturb you? Obviously, it has."

"Jennifer is always determined to get what she wants."

"And you think she wants you?"

He flushed. "I know that sounds conceited, but she acts as if she does. Last night, I remembered many things about our previous relationship. She always liked a challenge. It might sound less arrogant to say that she might not want me, but she's just curious to see if she can maneuver me into another relationship."

Carissa sat on the fireplace ledge and looked up at him. "It takes two to make a relationship. If you're unwilling to take up where you left off twenty years ago, I don't see why you need to worry."

He walked to the kitchen and turned on the faucet to draw a glass of water. "I told you Jennifer usually gets what she wants."

Carissa's eyes narrowed. "Are you afraid you won't have the willpower to resist her?"

Paul's face flushed again, and he drank a full glass of water before he answered. "That sounds rather cowardly, doesn't it."

If he was that fearful about Jennifer's attempts to snare him, was he as unaffected by her presence as he said?

"What do you want to do?"

"Avoid her. But I've come to the decision that I should go ahead and skate with her. If she throws any romantic lures my way, I can prove that I'm not interested by ignoring her."

"But what if you can't ignore her overtures?"

He shook his head, for he had no answer.

Carissa lowered her head, knowing that she had a similar problem. She wasn't sure she had the will-power to keep Paul at arms' length. If he kissed her again, how would she react? Just thinking about a romantic relationship with him caused her spirits to soar. And what if that thought became a reality? Her heart danced with excitement if their hands touched casually when they were working around the house. She wasn't sure he was affected, but she believed that if a web of attraction was building between them, she was powerless to prevent it.

She moved away from him and started to finish the interior decorations. Paul came over to help, and she sat on the steps while he stood by the railing as they decorated the stairway with garlands of poin-settias and evergreen.

Paul groaned when Jennifer appeared at the back door. She peered through the glass, saw them and entered without knocking.

With a short laugh, Jennifer said, "Paul, do you spend all of your time over here? Mother said that the apartment behind the house is your home. I've called several times without an answer."

"I'm seldom in the apartment and I *am* living here. When the three children invited themselves into Naomi's house, Carissa and I assumed responsibility for them."

"How long have the two of you known one another?"

"Since the day after Thanksgiving," Carissa said.

"Mother said you'd traded houses with Naomi."

Carissa didn't answer, and Jennifer turned her attention to Paul.

"We must talk about the skating party and our participation."

Carissa started to stand, but Paul put a gentle hand on her shoulder to keep her in a sitting position. She continued to wrap the greenery around the posts.

"I'm not interested in doing the exhibition. But Carissa and I have pledged to help Yuletide revive the spirit of Christmas. And since the skating party was once part of the celebration, I'll skate with you, but don't expect me to be light on my feet. I've skated sporadically over the past twenty years, so we can't perform a difficult routine."

"Then meet me at the skating rink this afternoon and we'll see how much you've forgotten. Two o'clock okay?"

"Let's make it one o'clock. Carissa and I are taking the children shopping when school lets out at three."

"How about having dinner together tonight to plan our strategy?"

"No. I'm committed to Carissa and the children every evening. We're trimming the tree tonight."

Shrugging, Jennifer said to Carissa, "Mother tells me that you're the owner of Cara's Fashions."

Carissa taped the last garland to the bottom step before she answered. "Not anymore. I sold the business two months ago."

"I've worn some of the clothes."

"Yes, I noticed that you had on one of Cara's sweaters yesterday."

Jennifer turned toward the door without saying whether she liked the clothes or not.

Carissa's comment about the sale of her business brought to Paul's mind his reluctance to become involved with a rich woman. But that point wasn't bothering him so much now. During his last conversation with his sister, Naomi had told him that when Carissa sold her company, she used a large portion of the income to establish a foundation for abandoned children. Not only was she not as wealthy as he'd feared, but her charity had convinced Paul that Carissa was a compassionate, caring woman.

"This must be our day for company," Carissa said, when the doorbell sounded at about noon.

A police cruiser stood in the driveway, and Paul opened the door for the chief of police.

Stomping his feet to get rid of the snow on his boots, Justin said, "Hiya! I have some news for you about the children."

"Come in. Got time to have a sandwich with us?"

"Sounds good to me. I worked all night and I'm finally heading home for some shut-eye."

Justin shrugged out of his heavy coat and laid it over the back of a chair.

"Is it good news or bad?" Carissa asked as she poured a cup of coffee for him.

"Not bad," he said, settling into a kitchen chair. "And for the good of everybody concerned, I think we'd better keep this information to the three of us until we decide what we want to do about it. If I tell one other person, including Belva, the news will be all over town by nightfall."

Paul set lunch meat, cheese and mayonnaise on the table. Carissa took a bowl of grapes and a loaf of bread from the refrigerator.

While they made their individual sandwiches, Justin said, "There was a message on the Internet last night about three missing children in Aberdeen, Vermont. The profiles sounded a lot like our Christmas children, so I telephoned the sheriff there. We had a long chat. There's no doubt we're dealing with the same kids."

A wave of disappointment spread through Carissa. Had she actually been hoping that the children couldn't be traced?

"Have they told us the truth?" Paul asked.

"Pretty much so, it seems. Their family name is Garner. Their mother was sick for several years and died about three months ago. The father hasn't been seen for several years. I gathered from the sheriff that the neighbors had been taking care of them for months."

"Is their family looking for them?"

"The sheriff said that a local preacher and one aunt had initiated the search. The kids are from a poor family. The extended family members aren't necessarily heartless, but none of them can afford to take in three children."

Carissa pushed back her plate. She'd lost her appetite. Her mouth was dry, and she swallowed with difficulty. "So, what do we do now?"

"The sheriff is going to contact the local welfare service, which has been supporting the Garners for several years. I told him of Yuletide's desire to include the children in our Christmas plans and that they are in good care. He thinks there won't be any demands to have them returned to their hometown before Christmas. They'll probably be put in foster care, though it's unlikely they'll find one family that will take all the children."

"So they'll be pushed from pillar to post?" Carissa said.

"More'n likely," Justin agreed.

"Shouldn't we tell the children what you've learned?" Carissa asked.

"That's up to you. I thought the kids should hear it from you rather than from somebody else." Justin stood, yawning. "I'm headin' for home, folks. I'll keep you posted on what I hear. Thanks for lunch."

While Paul chatted with Justin as he put on his coat and left the house, Carissa put away the food and placed their dirty dishes and silverware in the dishwasher. She went into the great room and absently picked up items that belonged to the children: Lauren's bear from the fireplace ledge, a book on football that Alex had been reading the night before and one of Julie's mittens lying on the couch.

When Paul returned he didn't interrupt her musings, but went into his bedroom to prepare for the afternoon's ordeal with Jennifer. Carissa was staring out the glass doors when he returned. He'd changed into a pair of gray sweats, and he sat on the couch to pull on his snow boots.

"I don't know whether I feel better or worse now that we've learned more about the kids," he said.

Carissa sat beside him. "I feel worse. There just doesn't seem to be a happy ending for them, unless I adopt them."

Impulsively, he laid his hand over hers—conscious, and relieved, that she didn't rebuff his touch. "No, Carissa, that isn't the answer. Haven't you seen enough already to know it wouldn't work? Where would you live? Would you take them back to Florida with you? It's too much for you to take on Lauren's physical problems, Julie's tantrums and Alex's stealing."

She looked at him quickly.

"Yes, he took ten dollars out of that billfold I planted in the basement. I hadn't seen any need to bother you with the knowledge."

"But don't you think they'd change a lot if they had the security of a home?"

"I'm not thinking about anyone but you. You've worked hard, and now that you're financially secure enough to retire, you ought to have a life of your own."

"But a life doing what? That's one reason I started thinking about finding Christmas. I didn't have anything else to do."

"Trust me, Carissa—this isn't the answer. You can find many worthwhile things to do without becoming a mother."

"You think I'm too old to do it," she accused.

"I don't think you're too old to do anything you want to. I'm not as old as you, and I wouldn't want to take on the single parenthood of three kids. I admit I've become attached to them, and I'd help you with them if I could. But in a few weeks, I'll be thousands of miles away."

He couldn't read her expression, but he didn't think he'd convinced her. "At least promise me that you won't make a hasty decision about this. Who knows—maybe their father will show up."

She looked at the clock. "You only have ten minutes to get into town."

Carissa didn't seem a bit disturbed about his association with Jennifer, so apparently Carissa wasn't experiencing the same feelings for him that had started infiltrating his mind and heart when he was with her.

"I'll meet you at the school by three o'clock," she said as he left the house.

Carissa seldom had any time alone anymore, so she took advantage of the peaceful moment to read the Bible. For years, Carissa had devoted all of her energy to making a success of Cara's Fashions, to the neglect of her spiritual nature. But since the pressures of business had been lifted from her shoulders, she'd tried to read the Bible every day. She was pleasantly surprised to find out how much she remembered of the spiritual truths she'd learned from the Bible as a child.

When she'd received such a large payment for her business, she'd recalled the Scripture verse, ''As we have opportunity, let us do good to all people.'' She'd pondered a long time about how she could do this, until she heard about an organization that was devoted to helping abandoned children. She'd felt that she should share some of what she'd gained, to help children who'd had the same misfortune she'd had.

Now, as she sat, Bible in hand, considering the Garner children, the story of Queen Esther came to mind. Esther, a Jewish slave girl, had become queen in the Persian Empire. Esther may have thought that she'd reached the pinnacle of success and that her life from then on would be one of ease. Yet, when her countrymen were on the verge of extinction, Esther had been told, ''And who knows but that you have come to royal position for such a time as this?''

Right from the first, Carissa had thought it strange that she'd been inspired to look for the meaning of

Christmas in a town she'd never seen, among people she didn't know. God's spirit was everywhere. Couldn't she have found the Christmas spirit in Florida? She didn't need to travel a thousand miles to find new meaning for her life.

Yet it seemed right for her to be in Yuletide, New York, in this house with Paul and the children. Had she, like Queen Esther, been brought to this locality for a specific purpose? During the few times she'd contemplated adopting the children, she'd always thought of doing it with Paul at her side. It seemed obvious that he had no inclination in that direction. And she could understand that he had a job to do. With Paul's cooperation she believed they could set up a happy home life for the Garner children. But where? Naomi would be returning to New York in a few weeks. They couldn't live in this house, which was too small for five people, anyway. Besides, soon after Christmas, Paul would return to Europe.

Could she handle the adoption alone? But would she *be* alone? If God had brought her to Yuletide because the Garner kids were here, wouldn't He be with her through parenthood as helper and guide? Queen Esther had had the prayer support of God's people to accomplish her goals. The local Yuletide church members had already demonstrated their willingness to help feed and clothe the children. She was sure that any church congregation anywhere would offer the same loving support.

But Paul had asked her to use caution, and she

would. She'd seldom acted on impulse, but since making the hasty decision to travel to Yuletide, she'd been jumping into troubled waters with both feet. Which way should she jump now?

Chapter Thirteen

Paul also felt the need for extra strength as he drove into Yuletide. He prayed for help in keeping his guard up against Jennifer's wiles. It wasn't his nature to be rude to anyone, but during this skating performance, he must keep their relationship on a strictly impersonal level.

He knew his task wouldn't be an easy one when Jennifer showed up at the skating rink wearing tights that looked as if she'd been poured into them.

"Oh, why are you wearing sweats? You'd be more comfortable in tights," she said, tapping him playfully on the shoulder.

"I'm not wearing tights until we're ready to perform. Besides, I *am* comfortable." He tied on the rented skates. "All I intend to do today is to learn how much endurance I have. I haven't been on skates for several months. You can explain what routine you have in mind, but we can't skate as partners today.''

Lifting first one leg and then the other, Paul tottered for a few moments before his body movements adjusted to the sensitive balance necessary for skating. Only a few other skaters were on the ice, and he spent several minutes circling the rink. He leaned forward, lifting his left leg and stretching it behind him, his arms extended in a straight line from his shoulders.

As always, he thrilled to the feel of the cold air drifting past his face as he glided across the smooth surface. Confident that he hadn't lost much of his agility, Paul tried a two-foot spin. With his feet slightly more than shoulder-width apart, he put his weight over his left thigh, his left toe gripping the ice. With his right arm pressed behind him, he positioned his left arm across his body, fingertips pointed behind him. He bent both knees equally, and with his arms held taut, he snapped his arms around and to the front, stretched his knees, straightened both legs, planted both blades on the ice, initiating the spin. He was pleased that he experienced only a slight dizziness, and decided he could probably do a creditable job of skating for the exhibition.

He glided across the glistening ice several more times, then experimented with cutting figure eights on the smooth surface. He tried several rotation jumps, and while he considered his movements clumsy, at least he didn't fall.

All during the practice session, he was aware of Jennifer. How could he help it when she circled him dozens of times? Her body was as youthful and glamorous as it had been when she was a teenager. When they made eye contact, she gave him a tantalizing smile as if to remind him of other times they'd performed together.

After a half hour, Paul's heartbeat was more rapid than he would have liked, so he skated to the side and sat on a bench. Jennifer executed a graceful waltz jump directly in front of him, then joined him.

"You haven't lost much of your grace," Jennifer said admiringly.

He rubbed his legs and went through a few stretches. "Maybe, but my muscles didn't appreciate the exercise." Hoping to hasten Jennifer's departure, he said, "I'll be here tomorrow at the same time, and we can work on our act. What routine are you considering?"

"Nothing too difficult. The last time we performed together, we skated to the music of 'The Tennessee Waltz.' For old times' sake, it would be fun to do that again. What do you think?"

"That's okay." He started to remove his skates, and Jennifer hovered over him.

"Then, how about going into Saratoga Springs with me now to choose our costumes? I have to make arrangements for the spotlights that have to be set up for the presentation, too. You could help with that."

Paul didn't want to spend any time alone with Jennifer, but several people were involved in various activities around the rink, so Paul indicated the bench beside him. "Sit down, please."

She sat close to him, her thighs grazing his. The contact was distasteful to Paul, but he didn't move.

"I told you earlier that I have other commitments this evening, and I intend to keep them. Before we go any further, I want to make one thing clear to you. Jennifer, I agreed to this performance because I want to see Yuletide glow with Christmas again. But I have no interest whatsoever in a relationship with you."

Her lips curled ironically. "You flatter yourself, Paul."

"Perhaps, but how else can I interpret it? You put me on the spot in front of the celebration committee. I had little choice but to accept your challenge."

"So you haven't forgiven me for breaking our engagement?" she said, her shoulders drooping pathetically.

"I don't know whether or not I have. But that's beside the point—it's in the past and I want it to stay there."

"You're making a mountain out of a molehill. I was so pleased to see you again that I thought it would be nice to skate together. Our practice sessions will be more pleasant if we're friends."

"No, Jennifer, I don't want to be your friend. You use your friends. We're acquaintances, nothing more."

"Have you fallen in love with Carissa Whit-more?" she demanded.

"I've known Carissa less than a month—it's a little soon to be in love with her. We've committed to take care of the children until after Christmas. That will take all of my time."

"Have fun, then," Jennifer said, and resumed skating. He didn't give her a backward glance as he turned in his skates, asked that they be reserved for him until after the exhibition, and left the rink. He doubted that Jennifer would give up so easily.

After they visited a department store and bought boots for the children, Paul suggested, "Anybody interested in eating out tonight? You're probably tired of my cooking, and I know *I* am. There's a special on hamburgers and fries at the café."

"Yeah!" Alex said, giving Paul a high-five. "The coach gave us a good workout in the gym today."

Julie grabbed Paul's hand. "The pastor said they're gonna make us do something in the parade."

Paul's eyes questioned Carissa as they got into the SUV.

"The pastor mentioned it to me," she said. "They want the children to be the town's guests and ride on a special float during the Christmas parade next week."

"That sounds like quite an honor," Paul said. "You want to be sure you deserve it."

He sensed rather than saw the suspicious glance Alex gave him.

Apparently the Garner children hadn't had many opportunities to eat in restaurants, but they were delighted to be able to order exactly what they wanted. Carissa asked Lauren to drink water instead of a soda, but otherwise, each child chose his or her food. When Alex ordered both french fries and onion rings, Carissa glanced questioningly in Paul's direction. He shrugged.

Carolers were singing along the streets of Yuletide when their meal was finished, and Carissa and her temporary family listened as the music faded into the distance. Paul and the children sang as she drove them home.

Once they were back, while the children went to their rooms with their belongings, Paul stepped near Carissa. "Are we going to tell them what we learned this morning?" he asked quietly.

She nibbled uncertainly on her lower lip. "I've been worrying about it all day, but I think we should. I'm tired of just thinking of them as 'the children.' We know their last name now, and I think we should use it. We're in the clear legally, since Justin has reported their whereabouts and gotten permission for them to stay here through the holidays."

Lauren brought a book downstairs with her and sat beside Carissa on the couch. Alex turned on the sports channel and was soon engrossed in a hockey game. Julie nestled down beside Paul, and he started reading a story to her.

"I read a book like this in my other school," Lauren said as she leafed through the pages.

Paul and Carissa exchanged glances, and taking a deep breath, he said smoothly, "Did you attend a big school in Aberdeen, Vermont?"

Julie apparently didn't notice the import of his question, but Carissa felt Lauren tense beside her. A dark, angry expression spread across Alex's face, and he stared at Paul. Obviously very disturbed, he turned off the television, his interest in sports interrupted.

"So you've been snooping around behind our backs?" he snarled.

Lauren started sobbing, and Carissa enveloped her in a tight hug. Paul's body stiffened, and he opened his mouth, no doubt intending a sharp retort, but Carissa shook her head.

"We did not snoop around," she said. "Chief Townsend received a bulletin yesterday that three children, with the last name of Garner, are missing from Aberdeen, Vermont. The children's first names were the same as yours, so he knew it was you."

"What'd he do about it, besides blabbing to you?"

"He did what he had to do," Paul said, trying to stifle the harsh words he wanted to say. "He contacted the authorities in your town and told them where you were."

"And I suppose they're sending someone to pick us up," Alex said bitterly.

"No. Justin told them we were taking care of you, and guaranteed your safety, which has been approved by the authorities in your area. There won't be any changes until after the first of the year."

"And then what?" Alex demanded.

"I don't know," Paul said, "but I wouldn't advise you to keep stealing money so you can run away again."

A hangdog expression replaced the anger on Alex's face, and he turned away.

"If the people of Yuletide have honored you by giving you a special place in the parade," Paul continued, "the least you can do is stop stealing from them."

Lauren's sobbing ceased, and she lifted a moist face. "Alex! You promised Mommy you wouldn't steal no more!"

"You'd have gone hungry more than once if I hadn't," her brother retorted without remorse.

"Stealing is never justified," Paul said sternly. "And I speak for Carissa, as well as myself—if you want any further help from us, you'll stop taking things that don't belong to you. I understand that you want to accumulate some cash to take care of your sisters when you're not with us anymore. But if you get caught stealing, you'll be in so much trouble that you won't be able to help anyone, not even yourself."

A look of despair spread over Alex's face, and

Carissa wanted to comfort him, but she knew Paul's method was needed now.

"You must return the money you took from the school to the pastor tomorrow. And I want the money you took from my wallet."

Alex reached into his rear pocket and took out a worn wallet. He passed over two five-dollar bills and a twenty. Paul felt like a heel for taking the money, but the boy *had* to stop stealing.

"The twenty is what I took from the school. Will you give it to the pastor?"

"No. If you're man enough to look after your sisters and mother, you're man enough to own up to what you've done."

Alex took the twenty and replaced it in his wallet.

"Now I know it isn't easy to be without money, and the three of you have been doing lots of work around here by bringing in wood and helping in the kitchen. I intend to give you an allowance for each week." He reached into his own wallet, replaced one of the fives, and took out some dollar bills. He handed the five back to Alex.

"Since you've done more work than your sisters, I'll give you five dollars a week. The girls will get two dollars each."

Alex turned the money over and over in his hand, and Carissa thought he was on the verge of tears.

"I'm sorry," he whispered, "but Mom told me to look after the girls. I'm not old enough to get a job, and I didn't know how else to do it."

Paul couldn't imagine why his mother had placed such a burden on Alex, but he supposed the poor woman was frantic, knowing she was dying and leaving her family without any help.

"If you're caught stealing, then who'll look after your sisters?" Paul asked.

Alex dropped his head into his hands, and Paul went to him and pulled him into his arms. Alex buried his face in Paul's shirt, his shoulders shaking with sobs. Julie slipped out of the chair and ran to grab Paul around the legs. He dropped his left hand to her head, while still holding Alex in the circle of his right arm.

Hardly conscious that she was speaking, Carissa said, "Stop all of this! I'm going to adopt you."

Three tear-striped faces lifted and stared at her.

"Carissa!" Paul said. "You shouldn't promise that."

Alex ignored his comment. "All three of us?"

"Yes. Legally, I don't know that I can adopt you, but I'll at least apply to be your guardian. It will take a long time, but perhaps I can be your foster parent until we see what we can do."

"Uncle Paul, too?" Julie asked.

Paul cast an angry look toward Carissa, as if to say, *Now see what you've done!* "Julie, I have to go back to my job after Christmas," he said.

Already Carissa was regretting her rash promise, but she couldn't stand the grief and fear these kids were obviously feeling. If she could do something to help them, for her own peace of mind, she had to do it. She was sorry that Paul was angry with her. Did he think she was trying to manipulate him into staying in Yuletide?

It would be so much easier if they could have joint custody of the children. She recognized how expertly he'd handled Alex tonight. She might be able to meet the girls' needs, but would she fail with Alex? She didn't know much about child psychology, but she believed Alex needed a father figure in his life. Paul had proven that he could provide that. Perhaps she shouldn't have promised. What if she made a worse mess of their lives than they'd had before?

She wasn't up to a confrontation with Paul tonight, so she said, "Girls, it's time for showers. I'll read a Christmas story to you before you go to sleep."

With a meaningful glance, Paul said, "Come down after the girls are in bed."

Carissa didn't respond. Paul was angry at her, and she was scared of what her impetuosity would lead to. If she waited until tomorrow, he might be over his anger.

She was halfway up the stairs, with the girls running ahead of her, when Paul spoke again.

"Carissa?"

She turned, unable to meet his gaze.

"All right. After the girls are in bed and I hear their prayers, I'll come."

"You gonna talk her out of adopting us?" Alex demanded.

''Carissa makes her own decision, but I think she's promised something she can't do. With your father missing, it could be years before anyone could adopt you.''

''But somebody will have to look after us until then. I can't think of anyone else who's willing to take us. Not even you.''

Paul could understand why Alex had a belligerent attitude, so he tried to explain. ''I'm a bachelor and probably wouldn't be allowed to adopt kids even if I wanted to. When I go back to my work, I'll be living in a shack about the size of the kitchen. The job is in an isolated area, without phones or television. A few men take their wives, but I honestly think the living conditions are too rough for women and children.''

Alex's expression, which had been so joyous when Carissa said she'd adopt them, was woebegone again. Paul gave him a quick hug. ''Don't start worrying about it. Carissa is a determined woman, and if she's made up her mind to adopt you, nothing anyone says will stop her. So take a shower and go to bed—tomorrow may be a new start for you.''

Paul's anger had cooled considerably by the time Carissa came downstairs. She paused uncertainly on the bottom step.

''Our talk can wait if you're tired,'' he said.

''Not physically tired—but emotionally I'm drained. If you want to bawl me out because you'd advised me against adopting the children, I'll save you the trouble. I admit that I shouldn't have spoken up as I did, but the children's grief got to me. I should have had a lawyer look into their situation before I promised them. I didn't build Cara's Fashions by giving in to my emotions, and I shouldn't have acted impulsively. But I did, so I'll live with it.''

He took her hand and led her to the couch. He turned off the overhead light, leaving only a small lamp to illuminate the room. When she didn't rebuff him, he pulled her gently down beside him, relieved that his temper was under control. Had he been angry because Carissa had spoken, or because she had alerted him to his own responsibility?

''My concern is for you. This is too much for you to handle alone. Your agreement with Naomi is for two months. Where will you take them after that? You'll have to establish a residence somewhere.''

''I have a house in Florida.''

''But when the state of Vermont has custody of our children, you might have to live there.''

''Don't ask me such questions. I have no idea what I've gotten myself into, and I can't even think about it. I've lived alone for years and I don't know what I'll do with three extra people in my home. Since I've been in Yuletide, I haven't had more than an hour to myself at any given time. That's frustrating. No wonder I'm making foolish mistakes.''

Paul remembered that Carissa had been reluctant to assume supervision of the children, and he'd more or less pushed her into it. "It isn't a mistake to have compassion for others, Carissa. It's a trait more of us should have." He moved closer and, wondering if he dared, drew Carissa into the shelter of his arms.

"It didn't seem as if I was the one who spoke," Carissa said softly into the fabric of his shirt. "It was almost as if God was speaking through me. I've read in the Scriptures that sometimes God puts words in our mouth. Deep down, I don't *want* to do this, but it seems to be the right thing to do."

He patted her back comfortingly. "I'll do what I can to help you as long as I'm here. I'll ask Justin to contact that sheriff again and learn everything he can about the children's father. In the meantime, we'll show them we love them and give them a Christmas to remember. You'll make a wonderful mother."

Pleased by his praise, Carissa stared up at him in astonishment, and the expression in his eyes made her heart beat very fast.

Her thick, curling lashes dropped in confusion. Paul touched her chin and lifted it upward. The pale gleam from the lamp lit her face with a dancing glow, and her eyes were very bright. A half smile hovered about her lips. Even as he bent closer, Paul struggled for control. He wanted to kiss her, but what if he upset her again? Emotional gravity seemed to pull them together, and when their lips touched in a gentle kiss, Carissa didn't pull away. Slowly her arms slipped around his neck, and she eased comfortably into his embrace. His heart thudded when he realized that emotions he'd thought he killed long ago were still alive and well.

The touch of Paul's lips brought an irresistible sensation to Carissa's heart, and she was happy at her own eager response to his gentle touch. Lying trustingly in his arms, she experienced no guilt. Once, she'd thought that to enjoy kissing and touching was immoral, but these few moments in Paul's arms had brought a new awareness that *real* love between a man and woman was more than sensual, it was also a meeting of mind and soul. After having known Paul for such a short time, could she possibly be in love with him? As incredible as it seemed, Carissa believed that was the case.

"Oh, Paul!" she murmured. Carissa eased out of his arms, not knowing that her eyes were glowing with an intensity that Paul found hard to resist. A rosy hue stained her cheeks.

As he watched the play of emotions on her face, Paul knew that his kiss had unlocked her heart. Carissa's lips parted in a smile as intimate as a kiss, and she studied his face feature by feature, her eyes dancing with excitement.

Paul was humbled to witness her metamorphosis from an emotionless woman to this vibrant, lovable person with a heart full of affection. Once he'd witnessed the emergence of a golden-winged butterfly from its cocoon. He knew now the same awe and unworthiness he'd experienced then.

"Thank you," she whispered.

"For what?" he murmured, his lips hovering in the soft curve of her throat.

"For making me feel alive. For letting me experience the kind of closeness I've often envied among other couples. For causing me to lose my misguided notion about the results of affection between a man and a woman."

"That kiss taught me several things, too."

Afraid to ask what he meant, unwillingly, Carissa stirred from his embrace and stood. "Why'd you ask me to come downstairs?"

He grinned sheepishly. "I've forgotten. But it was a good idea, whatever the reason. We'll talk about what happened in the morning. Good night, Carissa."

She sensed his eyes following her as she mounted the steps. Carissa felt as if she were dancing on clouds, and so intense was her perception of the wonderful thing that had happened to her that later she hardly remembered preparing for bed.

The next thing she knew, her pleasant dreams of Paul were interrupted.

"I tell you they were kissing."

Lauren's muffled words pierced Carissa's semiconscious state, and her eyes popped open.

The girls were tiptoeing their way to the bathroom.

"How'd you know?" Julie answered.

They entered the bathroom, but Carissa heard the

rest of the conversation through the partially closed door.

"I got up to come to the bathroom last night. The lights were still on downstairs. I peeked over the rail. They were on the couch huggin' and kissin'. It's the truth—cross my heart."

"Then that means we might get a daddy as well as a mommy," Julie said.

The relief and delight in the child's voice stunned Carissa. It took so little to bring hope to the children. And she feared it was a false hope. Regardless of their mutual affection, Paul had made it clear that he would return to work. There had been no mention of love—and she wouldn't marry someone who didn't love her. And now that they were so physically aware of each other, they couldn't continue in their present situation.

Chapter Fourteen

At the breakfast table, Lauren and Julie looked from Paul to Carissa and giggled intermittently.

"What's the matter with you girls?" Alex demanded crossly. He seldom awakened in a cheerful mood, and this morning was no exception.

Carissa thought the poor child had little to be cheerful about. For all of his grown-up airs, he *was* only a boy. And it had been a humiliating experience for him to be confronted with his thefts last night.

Paul's eyes sought Carissa's, and she shook her head. She'd have to tell him part of what she'd overheard, she supposed, though she didn't intend to tell him all that Julie had said.

In the few minutes that she had alone with Paul before he took the children to school, Carissa said, "Lauren saw us on the couch last night. She put two and two together and came up with five."

"I wasn't doing a lot of thinking at that time, but even if I had been, I'd have thought we had some privacy."

"I'm beginning to wonder if there *is* any privacy with three children in the house."

"I suppose not! We had to learn the hard way."

Feeling motherly, Carissa checked to be sure that Julie and Lauren were buttoned up securely against the cold weather. Paul stopped beside her as she stood at the door, and his eyes caressed her.

"Oh, well! Since they know anyway..." He stooped and brushed a gentle kiss on her soft cheek.

Tears misted Carissa's eyes as they drove away.

God, she prayed, *thank you for giving me this opportunity to* feel. *I didn't think I had any maternal instincts, but I believe I could love these children as my own. And though I'd successfully suppressed all romantic emotions, thanks for allowing me to meet Paul and be awakened emotionally by his caresses. Is it love I feel for him? Am I deluding myself to think that he shares my feelings?*

As the relationship between Paul and Carissa deepened, Yuletide moved full-speed ahead with its resurrection of the Christmas spirit. For three hours each night, a steady stream of cars passed the house, as people from as far away as New York City came to view the Christmas Fantasy.

The costumes for the progressive nativity were finished and the cast had practiced several times.

The skating show was scheduled for two nights before Christmas on the lake near Yuletide.

Paul didn't comment on his practice sessions, and Carissa was jealous of the time he spent with Jennifer. If he would only mention Jennifer, she wouldn't be so miserable about it. Carissa feared that he had succumbed to Jennifer's charming magnetism again, and he didn't know how to explain it to her.

She needn't have worried.

Now that Paul suspected he was falling in love with Carissa, he wasn't disturbed by Jennifer's ploys. She was a beautiful woman and he enjoyed skating with her again, but Jennifer was cold. Now that he'd uncovered Carissa's softness and compassion, he only had to draw forth her image as a shield between him and Jennifer.

Since the children would be the honored guests in the parade, Carissa and Paul took them into Saratoga Springs to outfit them for the event. Neither one of them had any idea about the clothes children liked, so they permitted the children to choose their own, reminding them that the clothes would be part of their Christmas presents. Obviously, the kids were expecting nothing; their delight in the new garments made it apparent that they'd have been pleased with nothing more. Paul and Carissa had already shopped for the children's other gifts. Remembering her own meager Christmases, and wanting to compensate for the Garners' poverty, Carissa would have liked to lavish gifts on them. She refrained, though, knowing that too much at one time wouldn't be good for their character.

When they were passing through the adult section of a big-mall store, Lauren paused beside a display of women's dresses. She lifted a maroon evening dress from the rack.

"Look, Alex," she said. "Wouldn't Mama have looked pretty in this?"

Alex ducked his head. "Don't talk like that," he said. "We've got to forget her."

Unaware that she was blocking the walkway, Carissa stopped and took Alex's hand. "Oh, no, Alex," she said. "Never forget your mother."

"If I think about her, I'll be crying all the time. I see the pretty clothes you wear and it makes me realize how little she had. I don't ever remember her having a new dress until the preacher's wife bought one for her to be buried in. She couldn't see it then."

He broke away from Carissa and ran to catch up with Paul, who was walking in front of them, holding Julie's hand. Paul hadn't witnessed the incident that had brought such misery to Carissa's heart.

Carissa's mother hadn't had many new clothes, either. She took the dress from Lauren's hand and hung it back on the rack.

"I miss Mama," Lauren said, tears forming in her eyes.

Carissa didn't try to stop Lauren's crying because she believed it was best for the child to weep away her sorrow. Besides, tears were welling in her own eyes. She took the child's hand and hurried to join Paul. She shook her head at the question in his eyes.

When Julie saw that Carissa and Lauren were in tears, she started wailing, and Alex turned away to hide his own sobs.

"What in the world happened?" Paul asked, bewildered, but he stooped to lift Julie with his left arm.

Carissa, blinded by tears, held to his right arm.

"Let's sit down on this bench," he said, moving out of the flow of mall traffic to a secluded area. Still holding Julie, he put his other arm around Carissa, who held Lauren's hand. Alex knelt in front of Paul, trying to quiet Julie, who didn't even know why the others were crying.

Carissa took a tissue from her pocket and blew her nose. "I'm sorry," she said between sniffs. "But Lauren saw a dress that her mother would have liked. Alex couldn't remember his mother ever having a new dress until a neighbor bought one for her burial. That reminded me that my mother didn't have nice things, either. I don't usually lose control, but I'm more vulnerable to my emotions now than I used to be." Forcing a smile, she said, "I'll be all right."

Paul felt like a drowning man grasping for a straw. He closed his eyes, praying silently for wisdom—he didn't know how to handle this situation.

God, I'm in over my head, going down for the last time. I need help.

"Looks as if you've got your hands full, sir. Anything I can do to help?"

Paul's eyes popped open, and he knew his face must mirror his astonishment. He glanced up at the tall, angular man standing before them.

"I hope so. The children's mother died a few weeks ago, and something in the store reminded them of her. What should I do?"

"Let them cry. Bottling up grief can be harmful. Tears can wash away a lot of misery. Are you their father?"

Paul shook his head, almost on the point of tears himself. "No, they don't know where their father is. My friend and I are looking after them for a few weeks."

The man glanced at the packages piled haphazardly around the bench. "Then I'd say you're doing all you can do. They need to know somebody cares for them." He shook hands with Paul and Carissa, gave each of the children a five-dollar bill and disappeared into the crowd of shoppers.

"He's a nice man," Julie said, a smile replacing her tears.

Paul prayed. *Thank you, God.*

The man hadn't done anything spectacular—nothing that Paul couldn't have done. But Paul needed some sign that what he and Carissa were doing was right, and God had sent His messenger to tell him.

"Is there anything else we need to buy?" he said to Carissa.

She shook her head, and handed Lauren and Julie tissues to wipe their faces.

"Let's have some food and then head for home," he said, thankful that they'd passed another hurdle in soothing the children's sorrow.

Carissa noted that Paul seemed to tolerate the practices with Jennifer, although each day, either by innuendo or by her sinuous movements, she tried to tempt him. She dropped by the house almost every day.

Paul asked Carissa to stay with him any time Jennifer came, and sometimes he wondered if he was afraid to be alone with her. But as long as he kept Jennifer's past actions in mind, and focused on his growing interest in Carissa, Paul felt confident that Jennifer was his past, not his future.

Paul put the letter in his pocket and walked out of the post office with foreboding. The message had come from his employer that the work project would resume the first of January, and that he was booked on an overseas flight from Kennedy International Airport, December twenty-seventh. Normally, Paul would have been delighted with the news because he enjoyed his job; he was usually ready to return to work long before the appointed time. But he'd been so busy with Yuletide's celebration, and being with Carissa and the kids, that the days had flown by.

With so little time left, he should go to see his sister, but he didn't want to leave his unofficially adopted family. And when he didn't want to be separated from them for a few days, how would he feel when he boarded the plane, knowing that it would be months before he'd be back in the United States?

Faced with this anxiety, he wasn't sleeping well. He paced around his bedroom in the dark, wondering what he should do. He believed he was in love with Carissa, and judging from his youthful feelings for Jennifer, he knew that his present emotions ran much deeper. His love for Jennifer had been more physical than true affection and admiration. Now he wasn't content unless he was with Carissa. Since their first kiss, he'd kissed her occasionally, and he knew she looked forward to his caresses. She often kissed him with her eyes, if their gazes met when the children were with them.

What would life be like if he married Carissa and became a father to the Garner kids? He'd been on his own for a long time. Could he so drastically change his habits without feeling trapped?

During one of his nocturnal musings, Paul looked out the window, amazed to see a man standing in the shadow of a spruce tree, watching the house. The next morning he checked the area and found many tracks, as if someone had watched the house more than once.

The person, whom he assumed to be a man, returned the following two nights. Paul became concerned enough to talk to Carissa about it. He'd learned that with three kids in the house, there were no secrets, so he didn't approach Carissa until he returned from taking the children to school.

"For the past three nights, someone has been watching the house," he said, "and I don't know how long before that."

At her gasp and startled look, he said, "I didn't want to disturb you about it, but you are a rich woman—do you think it might have something to do with you?"

"Oh, I'm not *that* rich," she protested. "If I lived twenty years in Florida without anyone having designs on my money, I'm surely safe in Yuletide. Could there be some connection with the children?"

"I've wondered about that," he admitted unwillingly. He didn't want to believe that the children were in danger. "I'll be out tonight practicing, and I didn't want to leave you alone without warning you."

"Should we tell Justin?"

"I can't decide. If the guy comes back tonight, I'm going to confront him."

"Oh, you shouldn't do that. Let Justin handle it."

"With all the visitors coming to town, Justin and his deputy have their hands full now, but I'll tell him what's going on, and that we'll notify him immediately if we need him. When I come back this evening, I'll put my car in the garage as usual, but instead of coming to the house, I'll stay outside and be on the lookout for our visitor."

"I don't like it," Carissa said worriedly. "But I'll

wait up until I hear you drive in. I'll flip the light on in your bedroom, and after about fifteen minutes I'll turn it off. Perhaps the guy will think you've gone to bed.''

''The times I've seen him, he watches from underneath that grove of spruce trees across the road. After you turn off the light, watch from my bedroom window. Or you can see just as much from the window in your bedroom. If I get into trouble, I'll signal you with my flashlight and you can call Justin.''

If Paul was attacked, he might not be able to give a signal, but Carissa didn't point out what must be as obvious to Paul as it was to her. Carissa still wasn't willing to put a name to her feelings for Paul, but she realized that she'd be devastated if anything happened to him.

But while Paul and Carissa were on guard, no one spied on the house that night.

After school was dismissed for the holidays, the children were at the house all the time. It was difficult for Paul and Carissa to discuss the situation or for Paul to get much rest. On December twenty-second, the day of the skating exhibition, Carissa took the children shopping to give Paul an opportunity to sleep.

''I'd like to go with you and the children,'' he said, ''but that skating routine is rigorous and I've been staying up late to watch, because I told Justin I would. I have to catch up today.''

"You might get more sleep in your apartment."

Carissa wondered if her concern was for Paul's rest, or if she just didn't want Jennifer to come to the house when Paul was alone. He didn't seem to have any affection for Jennifer; in fact, Carissa thought he simply tolerated her, but she was still dubious about Jennifer's motives.

"Good idea. And I'll leave my cell phone over here."

Broad-beamed spotlights highlighted the area of ice where the skating party would take place. Carissa had rented skates for the children and herself so they could participate in the general skating after the program. She'd never been graceful on the ice, although she'd done some ice skating in Minnesota as a child; she didn't think she'd forgotten how. Carrying the skates, the four of them found seats on the bleachers that had been erected along the shore of the lake.

Twenty acts, single and pairs, were entered in the competition. Three stern-faced judges had seats close to the ice. Paul and Jennifer's routine would be the grand finale of the program.

Booths were set up, with eager-faced youths selling hot cider and cocoa. The smell of popping corn permeated the crisp evening air, along with the scent from pine trees. Carissa sat on the bleachers, and sipped a cup of hot chocolate and watched "her" children mingle with the friends they'd met at school.

She was pleased that they'd adjusted so easily to a new life.

What would happen if they were forced to leave Yuletide and were sent to separate foster homes, or even forced to live with their father? If the man watching the house was their father, or even another relative, he would take precedence over her attempts at adoption. She should have talked to a lawyer, but in the pre-Christmas rush, she hadn't had time. If she waited until after Christmas, it might be too late.

Carissa enjoyed the amateur performances of the youthful skaters, but during Paul and Jennifer's routine, she was miserable. Jennifer was dressed in crimson tights, a short white cape over her shoulders. Paul's tights were light green, his cape bright red.

Their program lasted about ten minutes, every moment of which was agony for Carissa. When the music started, they performed separately, cutting figure eights in the ice, executing side-by-side solo jumps and spins. They skated in unison, close to each other. Once Jennifer got a lift from Paul that made her jump higher, longer and more spectacular. She landed gracefully, gliding backward on one foot. They did a spin by connecting their legs and whirling together.

The crowd cheered lustily when Paul tossed Jennifer into the air, watched her turn around and caught her. These feats executed, they skated to the center of the rink.

The volume of the music decreased as Paul took Jennifer in his arms, and they danced in perfect rhythm to the waltz music, dipping and swaying as gracefully on ice as if they were on a ballroom floor. Although the movements were rapid, sometimes they were so close it seemed as if only one body danced. The music stopped, and hand in hand Paul and Jennifer skated to the center to take their bows.

Well, she'd lost him! Carissa decided. No man would be stupid enough to want her when someone as clever, fascinating and beautiful as Jennifer Colton had set her cap for him. If Paul was in a position of comparing her and Jennifer, Carissa conceded that she wasn't even in the running. And if she lost Paul, as well as the children, her future looked bleak.

"Penny for your thoughts," Paul said. She'd been so engrossed in her worries that she hadn't heard him approach.

"It was a magnificent performance," she congratulated him. "Both of you skated perfectly as far as I could tell."

"Thanks. We didn't make many mistakes. It's easier than when we were competing. I was relaxed tonight." He took her hand. "Come on. It's time for you to skate."

"I'm waiting until the ice is full of people. Then, if I do a lousy job it won't be so noticeable."

She handed Paul the empty cup, which he took to the garbage can while she put on the skates.

When he returned he said, "I'll hold your hands until you get the feel of skating again."

How she wished he could hold her hands the rest of her life!

Carissa was wobbling from one foot to the other when Jennifer, wrapped in a white wool coat and looking unbelievably beautiful, stopped beside them.

"Oh, you're going to skate?" she asked Carissa.

Although annoyed that Jennifer had seen her awkward movements, Carissa forced herself to say sincerely, "Your performance was excellent. Congratulations."

"It was the most exhilarating experience I've had for years! I'm sorry now that I didn't continue my dreams and become a professional skater instead of getting married. But we don't always make wise decisions when we're young, do we, Paul?"

She fixed him with a predatory glance that worried Carissa.

"I made some good decisions in my youth, and I don't regret any of them. Let's go, Carissa."

"I'll see you shortly, Paul." Jennifer leveled a glance at Carissa. "I've invited all the participants to my house for a party, so I have to hurry and be sure the caterers have everything under control."

Since the children didn't have school tomorrow, Carissa had planned to have snacks when they got home and let them stay up later than usual. She'd counted on Paul being there, too, but she didn't betray that fact by her expression.

Paul held her hands to be sure she was balanced on the ice before he skated away to check on the children. It was so crowded on the ice, Carissa couldn't have fallen if she'd wanted to, but she didn't enjoy the experience. Her legs soon became tired from the unaccustomed exertion, so she went back to the bleachers, changed into her boots and huddled in her comfortable coat to wait for the children.

Brilliant lights focused on the gaily-garmented skaters—the scene reminding Carissa of a Currier-Ives painting. As she waited, she contemplated the past month. She'd come to Yuletide to find Christmas. How well had she succeeded in her quest? What had she really accomplished?

She'd found Paul Spencer—a man she admired very much. She'd taken three orphaned children into her home. She'd also found new purpose in life—at least temporarily—to replace the many years she'd devoted to Cara's Fashions.

But so much was still uncertain. She was afraid to adopt the children, even though she wanted to take them. Could she do it alone? With Paul helping, the task wasn't so difficult. Why couldn't she stop imagining how it would be if they were really a family— if she and Paul married and adopted the children?

Her fantasies about Paul had to stop. He'd opposed her adopting the children, and he'd made no bones about the fact that he was returning to Europe after Christmas. Although he'd been affectionate, and she believed he was attracted to her, he hadn't given the slightest indication that he intended to make a life-time commitment. And then there was Jennifer!

It had been agony for her to watch them skate together tonight. And she was honest enough to admit that her reaction was jealousy. Although Paul seemed indifferent to Jennifer's charm, how could he not have been affected by her nearness during the hours they'd spent perfecting that skating routine?

But even without Jennifer, was marriage an option? For one thing, she'd have to be sure that she loved Paul for himself, not as a way for her to adopt the children. Never until now had Carissa realized how she'd suppressed her maternal longings. When she'd decided not to marry, that had meant no children, so she'd subconsciously put aside any thoughts of motherhood. Now she was amazed to realize that she'd always wanted to be a mother.

If she did adopt the children, Carissa knew that she could rely on God to help her. If God put His approval on the adoption—and she believed that He would—she would manage.

"Why such a gloomy face?" Paul asked, halting in front of her with the children beside him. "I didn't know you weren't skating, or we'd have come sooner. Are you cold?"

"I'm very comfortable sitting here—much more than being out on the ice. I remembered the knack of skating but my joints and muscles didn't. Thinking about that long walk we'll have tomorrow night on the road to Yuletide's Bethlehem, I decided I'd better rest."

Their happy faces were answer enough, but she asked, "Did you kids enjoy yourselves?"

"I falled down and hurt my knees, but it was fun," Julie said, clinging tightly to Paul's hand.

Paul walked with them to her SUV, and after he checked to be sure the kids were buckled in, he looked in the window at Carissa, whispering, "I'll help take down the bleachers and other equipment now. Be sure and keep the door locked until I get home."

"I'll watch, and I'll be careful," she said. She wanted to caution him too, for she considered Jennifer a predator of the worst kind. If Paul went to her house, he'd be lucky to get home at all tonight. But Paul might not appreciate her advice. Instead of speaking, she stood on tiptoes and put her arms around his neck. Daringly, she planted kisses on his neck, face and lips.

As she jumped in the SUV and started the engine, she heard Paul gasp. Feeling heady, Carissa thought, "Let Jennifer deal with that!"

Chapter Fifteen

Thrilled by Carissa's kisses and the promises of the future they offered, Paul wished he could skip the party Jennifer had planned, but, not wanting to be a spoilsport, he'd agreed to put in a brief appearance. It took longer to dismantle the bleachers and the light equipment than he'd expected, and it was well after midnight before he was free. When he turned into the street where Jennifer's mother lived, he stopped abruptly. Not a single car was parked in front of the house. Could the party have broken up so soon? The porch light was on, indicating that the welcome mat was out.

Suspicion began to dawn in Paul's mind. Had Jennifer invited anyone other than him to the "party"? Suddenly, he was sure she hadn't. Anger burned in his heart that she would try to trap him.

As he looked back on the past, he remembered that

she'd invited him to a party the night he'd asked her to marry him. It turned out that he was the only guest then, too, and her parents weren't at home. Twenty years ago, he'd been gullible, but not now. Jennifer wouldn't deceive him again. He made a U-turn in the street, hoping she'd see him leaving. He was far more intrigued by what waited for him at his sister's house.

Carissa was watching from Paul's bedroom window when he drove in. She went to the rear door and opened it for him.

"I didn't know if you had a key," she said.

"Any trouble?" he asked.

She wanted to ask him the same thing, but she said, "I haven't seen anyone loitering about. Maybe the person was just looking at the Christmas lights. Our decorations have turned the house into a beautiful sight."

"I hope that's it." He shivered. "It is cold tonight. And it's going to be cold tomorrow night for that pageant. We'd better wear thermal underwear."

"I bought some for myself and the children last week."

"And I have some in the apartment."

She was annoyed at him. How could he stand there talking about underwear when she wanted to know how he felt about Jennifer?

Carissa drew the draperies over the sliding doors.

"I'm sorry to keep you waiting. I didn't go to the

party, but it took longer to dismantle the bleachers and spotlights than we'd expected.''

His words brought joy to Carissa's heart. Paul obviously hadn't fallen for Jennifer's charms.

On the other hand, he didn't have any plans for Carissa in his life, either. If she'd foolishly dreamed of a life with Paul, it was her own problem. He hadn't promised her anything.

The two-mile walk seemed long to Carissa, but as she and Paul walked slowly, she was conscious of the many people who stood along the road watching them. Paul played the part of the solicitous mate quite well. At times, he simply held her hand; other times, he circled her shoulder with his arm. He carried a walking stick, and swung it occasionally at an imaginary animal that menaced them.

They passed the knoll where the shepherds watched over the small flock of sheep. After a short interval they, too, would hear the angels' song and come to the manger. The three kings wouldn't leave their starting point until an hour after Mary and Joseph had departed. Slowly, they would wend their way on camouflaged horses toward the imaginary Bethlehem.

The sidewalks of Yuletide were crowded with onlookers, and the silence was almost unbelievable as Carissa and Paul walked slowly through the streets of the beautifully decorated town. Carissa saw their three children in the care of Belva Townsend, who'd volunteered to watch them during the pageant.

A huge electric star hung over the vacant lot beside the town hall where the false-fronted inn was located. But Carissa looked heavenward and nudged Paul to call his attention to the glittering star, millions of light years away, that hovered in the sky above Yuletide. It seemed to her that the star's radiance was a sign of approval of what they were doing tonight. Yuletide had indeed reclaimed Christmas. But had she?

Carissa and Paul were taken by the innkeeper to the stable, and after a short interval, Carissa appeared with the live baby in her arms. It was the first time she'd ever held one. The soft, cuddly infant felt strange, just as it must have felt for Mary when cradling her firstborn. Holding the baby gave Carissa an insight into what she'd missed by not bearing children. Perhaps she'd been wrong in her decision, but if she'd had a family of our own, she probably wouldn't be in a position to help the Garners. If God did indeed control the destiny of His creations, perhaps He'd kept her maternal longings bottled until this particular time for a reason.

As she sat beside Paul and waited for the remaining participants to find their places around the manger, Carissa thought of Zechariah and Elizabeth, the parents of John the Baptist. Elizabeth had been barren until long past the time for childbearing.

Although Zechariah and Elizabeth were righteous and kept God's commands blamelessly, they'd had no children. In Jewish culture barrenness was usually considered a curse for sin—a sign of God's disfavor. This childlessness must have been a lifelong disappointment. No doubt, they had prayed daily for a son and couldn't understand why God's answer was no.

But God intervened in their lives. Elizabeth had a son, John, who was destined to be the prophet who would prepare people for the coming of the Messiah. Their prayer was answered; their disgrace was wiped away in God's time. To be the parents of a prophet was a privilege greater than if they'd had a houseful of children.

Carissa was caught up in the pageantry. The way Paul squeezed her hand, when the shepherds appeared and bowed before the manger where she'd laid the child, she was sure he was experiencing the same emotions. A hidden choir sang ''O Come Let Us Adore Him'' during the adoration of the shepherds.

After the departure of the shepherds, the Wise Men came, their arrival heralded by the lyrics of ''We Three Kings.''

At the stroke of midnight, the crowds that had converged around the stable in the final moments of the pageant began to disperse. The mother came to reclaim her baby, and even though the manger was empty, Carissa had an uncontrollable urge to kneel beside that crude wooden structure. Yuletide had found the meaning of Christmas and so had she. Tears stung her eyelids when Paul knelt beside her and hugged her close to him.

Although she'd often doubted that she was where God wanted her to be spiritually, she knew now that she'd never forgotten what she'd learned that Christmas many years ago in Minnesota. Without Jesus in one's life, there was no meaning in Christmas. God had sent His Son to earth not to stay as a baby to be worshiped, but to die for the sins of humankind. Without the death and resurrection of Jesus, Christmas would never be commemorated, for there would be nothing to celebrate. The baby in the manger would have been forgotten long ago without Christ's death on the cross.

Had God been working in her life all along to prepare her to become the mother of the Garner children? It was difficult for Carissa to consider that God would single her out for this role. But she considered that as one of God's children, she had been chosen to carry out His purpose. She perceived the eternal truth that God wanted to give her every desire that was in line with His will for her life. Like Zechariah and Elizabeth, she only had to wait for the right time.

Once and for all, Carissa committed her life to God's Son. "Whatever Your will for my life, God, I accept it," she murmured aloud. "Please provide daily guidance on the path I should take."

Paul must have heard her words, for his grip tightened around her waist.

"God," he prayed quietly. "I, too, want to draw closer to you, make you an integral part of my life. You've given me the answer to many things these past few weeks, but I'm still uncertain of other decisions I need to make. My heart guides me onto a certain path that I don't think I can take. Don't I trust You enough for the future? Why can't I leave my life in Your hands? Please remove the veil of my uncertainty and show me Your way."

He knew what he wanted to do—but was it practical to do so? How could he quit his job and take on a family of four without the means to support them? No doubt Carissa had all the money they'd ever need, but he wanted to do his share. Paul had peace in his heart about his spiritual security, but the immediate future was still uncertain as he assisted Carissa to her feet.

"Come, my dear," he said. "It's been a long night. Let's go home."

At that moment, he wanted nothing more than to have the four walls of the house surround him, Carissa and the children.

Caught up in the excitement of the pageant, Paul had forgotten about the man who'd been watching the house. But long after Carissa and the children were asleep, he was awake, trying to make difficult decisions. Walking around his room in the dark, he chanced to look out the window. The security light's faint rays revealed a man standing again in the spruce trees.

"Enough is enough," Paul muttered. In the darkness, he struggled into his outdoor clothes, and without telling Carissa, he slipped out the back door. He had to approach the man from behind, and that meant crossing the road at some point. Using his flashlight sparingly, he walked a half mile north of the house, keeping under cover of the evergreen trees. When he was out of sight of the house, he crossed the road to the lake path. Walking quietly, he maneuvered toward the grove of spruce trees.

The man was leaning against a tree. As Paul neared, he jerked up his head and started running. With one big leap, Paul caught the man by the arm.

"No, buddy," he said. "You don't get away that easily. Why have you been watching our home?"

Paul became aware that the arm he held was scrawny and that the man was trembling. Compassionately, he said, "Come on into the garage. It's warmer in there, and we can talk."

The man didn't answer, nor did he resist Paul's iron grip, but Paul held tightly to his arm while they crossed the road and entered the garage. There were no garage windows facing the house, so he wouldn't disturb Carissa. He turned on the light because he wanted a look at his captive. Once inside, Paul released the man, who crumpled to the floor.

Frightened, Paul felt for a pulse, which he found readily enough. The man was a rack of bones—

whether from illness or malnutrition, he couldn't tell. After scrutinizing the unconscious man's face, Paul picked him up and carried him upstairs. The stranger was unshaven, but his clothes were clean enough, so Paul laid him on the couch. He raised the thermostat, and heat had already filled the room by the time he'd brewed some coffee. The man was stirring when Paul returned to the couch, and he shielded his eyes from the light.

Paul heard static on the intercom from the house. Carissa must have seen the lights.

"Paul," her frightened voice called.

"I'm all right," he answered. "I can't talk to you now, but please believe me, I'm in no danger. Go back to bed. We'll talk in the morning."

Sounding unconvinced, she said, "All right."

Since Paul had been taking his meals with Carissa and the children, there wasn't much to eat in his apartment. He found a half loaf of bread in the refrigerator, so he took two slices, toasted and buttered them. He carried the food to the table beside the sofa.

The man was sitting now, his head in his hands.

"Here, drink the coffee and eat some bread."

Without meeting Paul's gaze, the man lifted the coffee mug to his lips with shaking hands. He ate the bread hungrily. Pitying the man, Paul sat opposite him and watched. He supposed he was foolish to bring the man into the apartment. It was no wonder Carissa was worried. For all he knew, the man might have a gun. At least Carissa and the children wouldn't be at risk in the main house.

When the man finished, still not looking at Paul, he said, "Thank you."

"Well, let's have it," Paul said. "Who are you? Why are you here?"

"Keith Garner. I'm looking for my kids."

"It's a little late for you to be worrying about that, isn't it, Mr. Garner?" He wasn't surprised at the revelation, for Alex bore a marked resemblance to the man.

Keith Garner's haggard face flushed.

"How did you find out where they were?"

"A cousin of mine is the custodian in the sheriff's office in Aberdeen. I went back to town, not knowing my wife had died. I was beside myself when I learned the kids had run away. How did they get this far, and why did you and your wife take them in?"

"The lady isn't my wife." And at Keith Garner's stunned expression, he quickly explained why Carissa was living in the house. Paul briefly told him how they'd discovered the children in Naomi's house, and gave a brief rundown of how and why they'd run away. "What kind of a man are you that you'd desert your family and leave your children to cope with their dying mother?"

"I'm the kind of man who is more harm than good to them," he said bitterly. He pulled up his shirt-sleeves and revealed the evidence of multiple needle marks in his arms. "It started out with alcohol and mild drugs when I was a teenager, then I started using the hard stuff. I'd steal my wife's money to buy drugs, and I finally left, knowing she and the kids would be better off without me.''

Paul was angry at the man, but he detected remorse in his eyes. He could heap a lot of recriminations on Keith Garner for his neglect, but he suspected he couldn't say anything the man hadn't already said to himself.

''I've been in and out of a lot of rehab places, and they'd dry me out for a while. Then, I'd find a job and send some money to my family. I'd send it to my cousin and he'd take it to them as if he was providing it. I hoped they'd think I was dead, and I wish I was. The kids would be better off.''

''Julie doesn't even remember you, but Lauren and Alex think you're still alive. You must talk to them.''

Keith Garner half rose from the couch. ''No! I can't face them looking the way I do.''

''If you won't assume your responsibility as a father, at least make some arrangements to give them up for adoption. They're terrified that they'll be separated if Social Services get involved. Miss Whitmore has volunteered to adopt them. She's financially able to give them a home.''

''Are you and the lady going to marry?''

''I'm only in New York for a leave of absence from my job in eastern Europe. I'm leaving the country in less than a week. Carissa will do it on her own.''

"I'd feel lower than a snake to give my kids away, but I'm afraid to take them. My record is so bad, I can't get a decent job. People don't trust me, and I don't even trust myself."

"Mr. Garner, you have to see the children and tell them why you abandoned them."

"They're too young to understand."

"Believe me, Alex and Lauren have grown up mighty fast in the past five years. You can't walk out on them again without giving them some closure and making provisions for their future. Look me in the eye and tell me, man to man, if I can trust you to stay here in the apartment and see those kids tomorrow. It's the best Christmas gift you can give them. They're feeling very alone in the world."

Keith Garner reached out his hand to Paul, and Paul clasped it firmly. "I'll do what you ask. I'll be grateful for a warm place to sleep."

"Where have you been staying?"

"In the fishing huts on the lake at night and in the woods during the day. I've been here four or five days."

Taking in the man's lightweight clothing, Paul didn't know how he'd survived the cold weather. And judging from the pallor of his skin and the lackluster look in his eyes, Paul figured that Keith Garner was seriously ill. He knew he was taking a chance, but what else could he do? Perhaps he should guard the man all night, but first, he needed to tell Carissa what had happened.

"I have a disposable razor in the bathroom that you're welcome to use. I'll also lay out some towels and other things for you to use as you shower."

When he returned to the living room, Paul carried two heavy blankets. "I'll leave the heat where it is, so you should be comfortable."

"Thank you, Mr. Spencer. In spite of what you think, I do love my kids. I won't desert them this time."

Paul didn't lock the apartment. If Keith Garner had a mind to, he could get out. But in his condition, he wouldn't get far before the authorities picked him up.

Right now, he was more worried about Carissa than he was about the kids or their father. She didn't know what she was getting into taking on the responsibility of caring for three children, but she would be disappointed if Keith Garner took them with him. Paul hated to disturb her, but he doubted she was asleep, anyway, and he had to talk to her before morning.

Inside the house he took off his boots and went quietly upstairs. He could hear Julie and Lauren breathing softly as he tiptoed across their room. In the faint glow of the bathroom's night-light, Paul saw Carissa sitting upright in the bed, her hand to her throat.

He went close to the bed and whispered, "Come downstairs—we need to talk."

When she joined him a few minutes later, he said, "Let's go in my bedroom and close the door."

There he motioned Carissa to a chair and sat on the side of the bed. "The kids' father is over in the apartment."

Carissa gasped. "What!"

He put his hand softly on her lips in a bid for silence. "He's the one who's been watching the house. I saw him tonight and waylaid him. He's skin and bones, so it wasn't any trouble to confront him."

"Where's he been for five years? And how did he find out where the kids are?"

Paul told her briefly what Keith Garner had said.

"What have you done with him?"

He explained how he'd found Keith Garner and brought him to the apartment, and left him there for the night.

"Is that wise?"

"Probably not, but I couldn't turn him out into the cold. He's been sleeping in the fishing huts on the lake."

Carissa shivered and pulled her robe tighter.

"I don't want him to get away again. He's willing to let you adopt the children."

"Oh!" Carissa said, not knowing whether to laugh or cry.

"I still think it's too much responsibility for you, Carissa. Naomi will be back in a month. Where will you take them to live?"

"I don't know. I'm scared stiff, but I told them I'd adopt them if I could. I won't back out now."

Paul leaned toward her, and she lifted her face to

his. "They couldn't find a more wonderful mother," he said, "but I don't want you to do it."

It flashed into his mind that without the children, he could take Carissa with him on the job site. It was crude living compared to what she was used to, but he figured she would be able to cope with the rigorous life. He thought of the sightseeing they could do in Europe—almost like a two-year honeymoon. But would he still feel the same if they hadn't been involved with the children, who had seemed to give them a sense of closeness they might not have had otherwise?

"What kind of man is he?" she asked, interrupting his thoughts.

"He seems to have some pride, and he probably could have been a useful citizen if he wasn't addicted to drugs."

"Just like my mother. That's what started her downhill slide."

He didn't want her to start thinking about her mother. "I shouldn't have bothered you tonight, but I thought you should know before the kids did."

"I wasn't asleep, anyway. I heard you go out, and I was worrying about you. When I saw the lights on in your apartment, I was really scared."

"It's nice to have someone worrying about me," he said softly, taking her hands. She was so close and so desirable, but Paul set bounds on his emotions. He was in no position to offer Carissa anything except this moment. So he lifted one of her hands and placed a kiss in the palm.

As she left the room, Carissa felt a deep sense of disappointment. Paul would soon go out of her life, and she couldn't do anything about it.

Chapter Sixteen

They'd opened one gift each on Christmas Eve, but the thought of packages under the tree catapulted the kids from their beds as soon as it became daylight. Carissa hadn't had more than an hour of sleep, so she reluctantly left her warm bed to follow the girls downstairs to where Paul and Alex waited.

Paul and Carissa had agreed that they shouldn't go overboard in buying gifts, but each child had one large gift of clothing, and smaller gifts of books or games. They'd bought a piece of jewelry for each of the girls and a pair of skates for Alex.

Carissa's gift to Paul was a digital camera, and her box from him contained a diamond bracelet. Carissa's heart was touched by the gift, but her eyes promised Paul that she'd thank him properly when they were alone. His answering smile indicated that he understood.

"Let's pick up the paper and ribbons, then get dressed so we can have breakfast," Carissa said.

"Want us to take our presents upstairs?" Lauren asked.

Carissa shook her head. "No, let's leave them under the tree for now."

After the kids scampered to their bedroom, Paul said, "I'll check on our visitor. Shall I bring him over?"

"Might as well get it over with. If he's still here."

"Do we have anything the children could give him as a gift?" Paul asked.

"I bought a tin container of butter cookies that hasn't been opened. Would that do?"

"I should think so. Undoubtedly, the man hasn't had enough to eat."

"Should we invite him to eat breakfast with us?"

"Let's play it by ear—see how the children react to him."

Keith Garner was sitting on the couch watching television when Paul entered the apartment. He'd shaved, and trimmed and washed his hair. He'd tried to make himself presentable, and it helped that his clothes were wrinkled but not dirty.

"I helped myself to another slice of bread—hope you don't mind."

"Not at all."

"Have you told the children I'm here?"

"No—it will be a surprise."

"Maybe not a very pleasant one."

"I don't know. They've opened their Christmas gifts, and they're dressing now. In the meantime, let's talk. If you do let Carissa adopt the children, their future is secure. But what about you? You can't be more than in your late thirties. I hate to see a man throw his life away. If Carissa adopts the children, I can at least do something for you. I'll pay for a rehabilitation program for you at a good facility."

"It's too late for that."

Suspecting strongly that Keith Garner didn't expect to live long, Paul still insisted, "It's worth a try."

"I'll think about it."

Paul went into the bedroom and brought out a heavy coat that he'd worn when he was several pounds lighter.

"Try this coat on. It will be warmer than the one you have. I'm not in this country much in the winter, so it's practically new."

After spending a night in the warmth of the apartment, Garner appeared less haggard. Perhaps the children's first look at their father wouldn't be too shattering, but Paul figured that five years had made quite a change in Keith Garner's appearance.

When Paul and Keith stepped up on the deck, the children were sitting on the floor around the Christmas tree, examining their gifts. Carissa was working in the kitchen, and she looked up quickly when Paul opened the door.

Hiding Keith Garner behind him, Paul said, "Kids, you have another gift, too."

He stepped aside to let their father enter the room first. Carissa came from the kitchen as Alex jumped to his feet, his face flooded with a mixture of emotions that she couldn't figure out. He was such a bewildering boy. What if he rejected his father!

"Papa," Lauren cried, and she ran to him. "Mama died," she said, sobbing and clinging to the man, whose own cheeks were stained with tears. He patted her back.

"I know, Lauren."

Julie stared at her father as she sidled over to Paul and leaned against him. The questioning, lost look she turned on him threatened his composure.

"It's your father, Julie. Go speak to him."

While she hesitated, Alex, who'd been standing like a statue, turned an angry look on his father. "Where have you been?" Alex said defiantly. "Mom wanted so much to see you before she died. I hate you."

"I don't blame you, son. I hate myself."

"Let's sit down," Paul said. "Your father has a few things to tell you. Mr. Garner, this is Carissa Whitmore. She's been looking after the children for about a month."

"For which I thank you, ma'am."

When they sat down, Carissa coveted Julie's position in the safe harbor of Paul's arms. She felt alone and vulnerable. Lauren sat in the chair beside her father. Alex stood in front of the fireplace, his back to the rest of them. A tense silence surrounded them.

Awkwardly, Keith Garner cleared his throat, and his hands moved restlessly on the arms of the chair he occupied.

"I've been a drug abuser since I was a young man, and I was too weak to break the habit. Anytime we had trouble of any kind, I'd forget my worries by taking drugs. It finally got me."

The two daughters obviously didn't comprehend what their father meant. But the bleak look on Alex's face as he glared at his father indicated that he knew all too well what kind of life his father had led.

"Don't you see, son? You were better off without me. When I was at home, I'd use all of our money to feed my habit. You were better off without me," he repeated, his eyes begging for understanding.

"If you really cared, you could have kicked the habit," Alex said.

"Alex," Paul said, "you don't know what you're talking about. You've never walked in your father's shoes. Try to be more understanding."

"I've tried, Alex, I really have. I've been in and out of a dozen rehab centers, and I'd go straight for a while."

"And that's when you sent us money?"

Keith Garner nodded. "But the addiction was too strong for me. With my record, it got harder and harder for me to find a good-paying job, and I didn't have much money to send your way."

He started coughing and gasping. Paul put Julie aside and went to Keith. The children stared in horror as their father struggled for a breath, and Carissa wondered if they'd have been better off not to have seen him.

"Shall we have some breakfast? Maybe some hot coffee will help you," Paul said.

Carissa bolted out of her chair, glad to have something to do. "You'll eat with us, please, Mr. Garner?" she said.

He was weak from the coughing spell, but he said, "Thank you. Something hot to drink would be fine."

Paul pulled chairs around the table for the six of them and got everyone seated while Carissa put frozen waffles in the toaster. She poured orange juice, and filled Mr. Garner's mug with coffee, which he sipped gratefully.

Lauren eyed her father nervously all through the meal. He ate very little, but he asked for another serving of coffee. Paul didn't think anyone enjoyed the meal, for Keith Garner was uneasy, the children's insecurity had surfaced, and Carissa was edgy. When he invited the Garner family to return to the great room, he, too, was doubtful about the outcome of the reunion between this man and his children.

Carissa had been fretting about their Christmas dinner before the appearance of Mr. Garner, and she hardly knew what she was doing. Leaving Mr. Garner alone with his children for a while, Paul put a ham roast in the oven. Carissa prepared a packet of dressing, knowing that her grandmother would have been horrified that she hadn't prepared it from scratch. She'd bought a cranberry salad, pumpkin pies and yeast rolls at the deli—all no-no's to her grandmother, who'd probably never heard of a deli. But Carissa was grateful for the advanced technology today, for her emotions were so mixed that preparing food was the furthest thing from her mind.

Would Keith Garner agree to let her adopt the children? What would happen to them if he decided to take his children with him? In less than a month, Carissa's life had become so involved with the three kids and Paul that she couldn't contemplate the future without them.

Perhaps sensing her confusion, Paul pulled her into a close hug.

"Everything is ready," he said. "I've peeled the potatoes, and they'll cook slowly while we wait for the ham to bake. We might as well get this over."

Carissa took the tin of cookies with her into the great room, where the children were showing Keith Garner their Christmas gifts. Lauren and Julie were chatting easily with their father. Alex had thawed to the point that he was sitting on the floor beside his father's chair, and Keith had his hand on Alex's shoulder.

"Lauren, would you like to give your father a gift?" Carissa asked, handing the box of cookies to Lauren.

Julie jumped up. "I want to give it to him," she said.

"Why don't both of you hold it?" Carissa said.

Keith's head bowed over the gift. "Thank you," he mumbled, and a sob rose from his throat.

He lifted his head and looked from Paul to Carissa.

"And I thank both of you for what you've done for my children. It gave me nightmares to think that they might have fallen into the wrong hands. If there is a God, I pray that He'll bless you for what you've done."

"There *is* a God, Mr. Garner," Paul said. "I've always believed that, but my belief was renewed last night when I again met the Son of God, Jesus, in a life-changing experience. He's already blessed us by giving us the opportunity to care for your children. Now the question is—where do we go from here? I'm sure the three adults in this room want the same thing—what is best for Alex, Lauren and Julie."

"I understand, Miss Whitmore, that you want to adopt my children," Keith said.

"I told them I would adopt, but that was before we knew you were still alive."

"I love my children," he said sincerely, "but they'd have a worse life with me than they had when their mother was ill."

"We'd take care of you, Dad," Alex said, standing at his father's side.

"I know you would, Alex, but I can't ask it of you. I don't know Miss Whitmore's position, but it's obvious she can give you the things I can't. A comfortable home, food on the table, nice clothes, a college education, maybe even love...." His voice trailed off, and he looked at Carissa expectantly.

"Yes," she said simply. "I love the children already. I've worked most of my life establishing a good business and I've never married. I didn't know my life lacked anything until this month. Being with your children has brought a completeness to my life that I've never known before. To be honest with you, I don't know what kind of a mother I'll be, but in many ways, I can empathize with the children. My mother died when I was a girl, I never knew my father and my grandmother raised me. I know what it's like to be alone."

"Kids, you need to be involved in this decision," Paul said. "What do you want to do?"

"I want to stay with Miss Cara, but I want Papa, too," Lauren said.

"That's what I want," Julie shouted. "And Uncle Paul, too."

Paul knelt beside her, his face white. "Julie, I've explained that I have a job. I still want to be a part of your life, but I have to work."

Alex looked at Carissa. "Can't we just go ahead and live with you without you adopting us?"

Taken aback by this turn of events, Carissa hesitated.

Before she could answer, Mr. Garner said, "No, it won't work, Alex. Miss Whitmore has to have full authority if she takes you. I don't want to be in a position to undermine her decisions.'' He turned to Paul. ''How soon can we sign the necessary papers?''

''I know nothing about adoption procedures, but there's a lawyer in Yuletide who handles my sister's affairs. He'll be able to advise you. I'll try to get an appointment for tomorrow. I've heard that adoptions usually take a long time, but since both you and Carissa are agreeable to this, there shouldn't be any hitches.''

Paul invited Keith Garner to stay in his apartment until they could find more information, so Keith went to retrieve his backpack from one of the fishing huts on the lake, and Alex went with him. Paul wondered if Alex wanted to keep his eye on his father, fearful that he'd disappear again. When they brought the pack to the house, Paul judged that it didn't weigh more than ten pounds. Was this all Garner had to show for a lifetime? No wonder he wanted something better for his children.

Keith asked Carissa if he could wash some clothes, and he and Alex spent time alone in the basement taking care of that chore.

Carissa hoped they were able to do some bonding as father and son. Alex needed to forgive his father.

After Paul arranged an appointment with a lawyer for the morning, he telephoned Belva Townsend, asking if she'd come to the house and stay with the children while they were with the lawyer. At the office the lawyer explained the adoption rules, and Keith Garner signed the necessary papers to initiate the proceedings. Carissa gave the lawyer permission to check her financial standing.

Knowing that Belva would take care of the children, after they left the lawyer's office the three of them went to the café for lunch.

"I hope Alex won't give you any trouble, miss," Keith said as they waited for their food to be served. "I don't want him to take after me."

Secretly, Carissa had been hoping the same thing. She believed she could cope with the girls' problems, but she knew nothing about boys. Despite the fact that he'd abandoned his family, during the few hours she'd spent with Mr. Garner, Carissa had formed a better opinion of his character. Still, he'd admitted in front of his family that he'd started using drugs and alcohol when he was a teenager. Bitter as Alex was about his family life, would he follow his father's example? The possibility sent shivers of fear up and down her spine.

"I'm going to give Alex a good talking-to," Keith said.

"But what about you, Mr. Garner?" Paul said. "Even if you are no longer legally responsible for them, you're still their father, and they'll want the best for you. It's obvious you are ill. For the children's sake, if not for your own, why don't you see a doctor? I'll pay for the initial tests, and if you need further treatment, I'm sure you'll be eligible for financial help.''

After some hesitation, Keith said, ''I've tried to keep going because of my kids, but now that they'll be taken care of, I don't really have much to live for. But if you think it will help them for me to stick around a little longer, I'll do it. Besides, I'll need to stay close by, so I can sign the adoption papers when they're ready.''

''Good!'' Paul said. ''I have a flight out of Kennedy tomorrow night, so I'm leaving early in the morning. If you'll go with me, I'll drop you off at a hospital in Saratoga Springs and make the necessary financial arrangements for you to be admitted.''

''I appreciate it. You know, I've never had much use for religious people because I've never been able to tell the difference between people who profess to be Christians and the ones who don't. But I've been wrong. I've looked in the wrong places to find Jesus in people. The preacher and his wife in Aberdeen looked after my kids, and the church members paid for my wife's funeral. I'm a stranger to you, but you're willing to pay my hospital expenses. And Miss Whitmore is adopting my kids, although she's scared to death to do it.''

Carissa gasped and felt her face flushing. Was it that obvious?

A slight grin appeared on Keith Garner's face. ''I shouldn't have mentioned it, but it's normal for you to be afraid to take on a job like this. Are you sure you want to do it?''

''It's too late to back out now, and I *do* want to take your children. I only hesitate because I'm not sure I'll be the kind of guardian they need.''

''When I was a child, my mother took me to Sunday school, and I remember the preacher saying that 'Jesus went about doing good.' I'm seein' that in the two of you.''

''Oh, no!'' Carissa said. ''I'm not worthy to be compared to my Savior.''

Paul covered Carissa's hand with his. ''Remember the story we talked about a few weeks ago? The people who'd heard that Christ was coming to visit them missed their opportunity by turning away several needy people because they were waiting for Christ. You came to Yuletide seeking Christmas, and you've found Him by opening your heart to others. When we sacrifice to help others in need, we're doing what Jesus would do. Don't you see, Carissa? You've found Christmas through the Garner children.''

Tears filled in Carissa's eyes and eventually found their way down her cheeks. ''Yes, I suppose I have. With God's help, I'll do the best I can for your children, Mr. Garner.''

''I've never doubted that for a minute, or I wouldn't have agreed to this adoption.''

Painfully aware that this time tomorrow night they'd be separated, after dinner, Paul and Carissa left the children alone with their father and took a walk along the lake on a path not illuminated by the Fantasy lights.

"I suppose I'm feeling motherly already," Carissa said. "I'm uneasy about leaving the children with him. What if he decides to steal them from us?"

"That worries me, too, but he is their father. I thought we should give them some time together. I believe that he wants the best for them."

"Do you think he has a communicable disease?"

"No. I don't believe he would be around his children if that were true," Paul replied. "But I wouldn't be surprised if Keith Garner knows he has a terminal disease, and that he's trying to provide for the children while he's still alive. Let's forget them for a few minutes. I had to have you to myself for a little while tonight. I can't believe that tomorrow night I'll be gone."

Soft snow covered their shoulders as he leaned against a towering evergreen and pulled Carissa into the circle of his arms. "I love you, Carissa. It must have been love at first sight. I don't know what was in that poker you used to whack me on the head, but it was as powerful as Cupid's arrow."

She laughed softly. "I love you, too. It's such a strange feeling for me because I've loved so few people. Only my mother and grandmother, now you and the children. It's rather scary to be overwhelmed with love for another person."

He cupped his hand around her face and held it

gently. "I can't bear the thought of leaving you tomorrow."

"Then stay here."

"Don't tempt me. I want to marry you and adopt the kids with you, but I won't live on your money. If I had another job comparable to what I have now, I wouldn't hesitate a minute. But overseas work is profitable and I can retire after twenty years of service. I can't throw all that away."

"How long before you retire?"

"Two years."

"How much do you love me?" she asked.

"Enough to want to marry you."

"Then delay your flight until we can get married and you can take the kids and me with you."

"I've considered that, but I don't think we could take the children out of the country with the adoption pending." A thoughtful expression crossed his face, and his brown eyes gleamed with eagerness. "And don't think I'll marry you and leave you behind!"

"Then, we'll come to you as soon as their adoption is complete. We can get married when I arrive."

Paul thought of his reservations about the living conditions on the work projects. But the pleasure of having Carissa and the children with him overturned his concerns. "You'd be willing to do that?"

"I'll do it in a heartbeat, Paul. Besides the fact that I don't want to be separated from you, I need you. It hasn't been too difficult with you here, but

I'm terrified to face all the children's problems alone. And I know there will be problems.''

''It's an option, certainly, and something that will make my leave-taking a little easier. Several of the engineers on our job take their families with them, so it isn't impossible. I'll look into it.''

He picked Carissa up and swung her around and around.

''Stop it, Paul. I'm getting dizzy!''

''It's just that I haven't been able to see any possibility of marrying you, and now there's a light at the end of the tunnel.''

Paul's brown eyes held great tenderness. Reveling in the feel of his arms so close about her, Carissa said brokenly, ''I'm going to miss you.''

Paul whispered his love for her even as he claimed her lips. At length, he rested his head against her soft hair.

''The time will pass quickly, love. We'll find a way to be together. I promise you.''

Paul's pickup was parked in front of the house, and the children were outside saying a final goodbye to their father as he stepped into the truck.

Paul stood in the foyer of the house, and Carissa was weeping in his arms. His eyes roved over the room where they'd been so happy.

''My dear,'' he said, ''God will provide some way for us to be together. We've committed our lives to Him—we mustn't underestimate His power.''

"That's the only comfort I have—knowing that God will help me with the children until you come home again."

Carissa stirred in his arms and broke their embrace.

"I feel like a heel, leaving without seeing my sister, but there wasn't enough time to coordinate my schedule with hers," Paul said.

"I'm sure she'll understand."

"I tried to call Naomi again this morning," Paul said. "I thought she would have returned from that cruise. I'll try to reach her after I'm checked in at the airport."

"If she calls after you leave, I'll tell her to expect your call."

"Well, I can't delay any longer."

He led Carissa to the door, his arm tight around her. She lifted her lips and he kissed her hard. She sobbed when the phone rang.

"Please answer it," she said. "I can't talk to anyone right now."

Unwilling to lose a minute with her, Paul drew Carissa beside him toward the ringing phone. He peered at the caller ID.

"It's your phone listing," he said. "It must be Naomi!"

He lifted the receiver and pushed the audio button so Carissa could hear.

"Hey, sis," he said. "You almost missed me. I'm ready to step out the door."

"I called as soon as I could. Our group traveled back from Tampa to Miami by bus. On our return trip last night, the bus had engine trouble and we didn't get home until fifteen minutes ago."

"A belated Merry Christmas, sis."

He held the phone toward Carissa.

"And Merry Christmas from me, too," she said. "Did you enjoy the cruise?"

"Oh, it was wonderful!" Naomi said, and Carissa thought she seemed very bubbly for a woman who'd spent the night on a bus.

"Paul, I've never been so happy. I'm going to get married."

Paul almost dropped the receiver. "What!"

"Don't you approve?" Naomi said, disappointment in her voice.

"It's not up to me to approve or disapprove. I'm surprised, that's all!"

"I'm surprised myself. I never intended to marry again."

In an excited voice, Naomi said that she was going to marry John Brewster, the man from Wyoming who'd been so friendly to her. "We didn't know we were in love until we were on the cruise. It was so romantic. Aren't you happy for me?" she added.

"Of course," Paul said. "But isn't it a quick decision? You've only known this man a month."

Carissa playfully nudged Paul in the ribs. He looked quickly at her, and she stretched to brush his lips with hers.

"Love often comes on swift wings," Naomi said, and Paul chuckled merrily.

"I agree with that," Paul said, and as Carissa's fingers caressed his face, he pressed a kiss on her hand.

"What about the children?" Naomi asked.

"They're still here—"

Before he could explain further, Naomi said, "Paul, I'm glad I caught you before you left. I have a proposition for you. Can I persuade you to take over management of the mill for me? I'll give you twenty-five percent of the stock, and you set your own salary."

"What!" Paul's voice was incredulous.

"You know I've never been happy managing the textile mill—it's been a burden to me. John lives in Wyoming six months of the year. I want to move there with him, and in the winter come back to Tampa. But that mill is my only income, and I need someone I can trust to manage it."

If Paul ever had needed confirmation that God was in control of his life, he had it now. He made up his mind quickly—or perhaps God had already made it up for him. As part owner of the mill, he'd have financial security, so he'd have no hesitation about leaving his engineering job.

"I'll do it, if you'll sell me additional stock so that I'll own forty percent of the company. And," he added, smiling, "if you'll agree on Carissa working with me as a consultant. She has more business experience than I do.''

''But she's retired—she doesn't have to work.''

Paul's eyes darted toward Carissa. She nodded agreement. She could certainly combine her parenting responsibilities by working part-time at the mill. Especially if Paul was by her side.

''You aren't the only one who's fallen in love. Carissa and I are going to be married, too.''

''Oh, that's wonderful news!'' Naomi said. ''You've missed so much happiness living alone.''

''Well, I won't be living alone much longer,'' he said with a laugh. He would wait until later to pass on the news about their ready-made family.

Naomi yawned audibly. ''I'm too sleepy now to talk about the nitty-gritty details. I just wanted to get your agreement before you left the country—Carissa, are you still there?'' she asked.

''Yes.''

''I'd love to stay in your condo the rest of the winter. John won't leave for Wyoming until the last of March. Are you interested in continuing our arrangement for a few more months?''

''Yes, that would work for me, too.''

Paul replaced the receiver and enveloped Carissa in a hug that threatened to crack her ribs. The touch of his lips was like a promise.

When he finally lifted his head, Carissa felt protected, loved and desired. Wrapped in the security of his love, she was speechless, but she still had enough breath to whisper, ''Let's go tell the children.''

Epilogue

Four years later

Paul and Carissa sat hand in hand, as Alex took his place among the graduating seniors. When he walked on the platform to receive his high school diploma, Paul whispered, ''Whew!'' and wiped imaginary sweat from his forehead. His clownish gesture hid the pride he felt for his adopted son.

Alex had already been accepted on a sports scholarship at a state university. To have gotten the willful Alex this far was evidence that they'd done a pretty good job of parenting. Who'd have thought that the undernourished, tense, gangly boy they'd taken in would develop into this tall, handsome youth who walked with catlike grace.

Julie sat with her hand resting on Paul's arm, for

the years had not lessened the bond that had been forged at their first meeting. At ten, she was a happy-go-lucky girl with lots of friends, although her grades left much to be desired.

Lauren sat at Carissa's left. A quiet, tenderhearted girl, Lauren was a superior student, and now that she was happy and secure, her fragile beauty won the affection of her peers, as well as many adults.

Although mothering the children had often tried Carissa's nerves, she'd never spent more rewarding years. After Paul had agreed to take over management of the mill, he'd returned to his job in the Czech Republic for two months to give his employer time to find a replacement. The short separation, which had seemed like years to Paul and Carissa, had provided enough time for them to realize that their hasty decision was the right one. They were married as soon as he returned to the States.

By that time, Naomi's lawyers had drawn up the necessary papers for Paul to take over the management of Townsend Textile Mill. They'd established their permanent residence in Saratoga Springs, but they'd traded Carissa's Florida condo to Naomi in return for the house on Lake Mohawk. They spent the summer months, as well as the Christmas holidays, at the lake house. Participation in Yuletide's Christmas festivities was a highlight of their family.

By the time Paul had come back from overseas, Jennifer Colton had apparently given up forging a new relationship with him; she'd sold the family home in Yuletide and taken her mother to New York. She hadn't returned.

Mr. Garner died a few months after the adoption proceedings had been completed. The children had made weekly visits to him in the hospice, and these visits had solidified their relationship. Having those months with their father had reconciled them to his illness. And he'd also been instrumental in steering Alex on the right path. Paul and Carissa had arranged a funeral for the children's father, and his body had been taken to Vermont for burial. A granite marker was erected to mark the graves of both parents.

The ceremony now over, Alex headed in their direction. Paul greeted him with an affectionate grip on the shoulder, and Carissa hugged him and stood on tiptoes to kiss his cheek.

"We're proud of you, son," Paul said.

Alex ducked his head in embarrassment. After clearing his throat a couple of times, he thrust his diploma into Carissa's hand.

"I don't say thanks very often, but all during the program, I kept thinking of where I might have been if you guys hadn't taken me in. You earned the diploma, not me. Thanks."

Paul and Carissa exchanged a look of satisfaction and surprise. More than once, they'd wondered if their children had any comprehension of the sacrifices they'd made for them. But they'd been repaid over and over for anything they'd given up.

Carissa had come to Yuletide to find Christmas,

but she'd found so much more—an affectionate husband, a loving family and a closer relationship with her Lord.

*   *   *   *   *

Dear Reader,

I'm writing this letter in mid-December, and the hustle and bustle of the holiday season. Since this book has a Christmas theme, and since my hero and heroine take on the role of caring for three orphaned children, it seems fitting to consider the role of Joseph and Mary in the incarnation of Jesus.

Mary willingly submitted when God chose her to be the instrument to fulfill His promise to Israel and to the rest of the world. She set aside her own plans and rejoiced, even though this acceptance might have led to alienation and shame. Joseph also responded with faith and understanding to God's plan. It must have been disturbing news to him that Mary was going to bear a child, and Joseph also ran the risk of being ridiculed by his peers, but he nevertheless accepted the message from the angel as God's will.

Like Mary and Joseph, the main characters in *The Christmas Children,* Carissa and Paul, had to make drastic changes in their lives to provide for the children who came to them during the Christmas season. It took faith and dedication, for as with Mary and Joseph, the "when and how" was not laid out for them. When they accepted God's will, they stepped out on faith that what God had initiated, He would bring to completion.

Often God calls us to a particular commitment. Our response to that message may bring with it joy or sorrow, but how blessed we are when we accept that plan that God has for our lives, not just at Christmas, but throughout each day of the year.

May God bless you.

Irene B. Brand

HEAVEN'S KISS

BY

LOIS RICHER

A run-down ranch and a mountain of debt were all Danielle DeWitt had left of her father. But her unlucky streak seemed to end when Dr. Lucas Lawrence entered her life, saving the town's play. Could Danielle convince the commitment-wary interim physician that he belonged in small-town Blessing…permanently?

Don't miss

HEAVEN'S KISS

On sale January 2004

Available at your favorite retail outlet.

Visit us at www.steeplehill.com

LIHKISS

Still Waters

A stunning debut novel of love, intrigue and newfound faith.

Gang terror shatters the sleepy town of Lakeview, Virginia, and Tiffany Anderson suddenly becomes the target of a violent crime.

Can Sheriff Jake Reed move beyond the hurts of his past to solve the crime and save the woman God has meant for him?

SHIRLEE McCOY

Available in January 2004, wherever books are sold!

Steeple Hill®

Visit steeplehill.com

SSM510

Love Inspired®

WHAT THE HEART KNOWS

BY

MARGARET DALEY

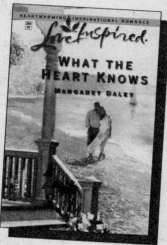

Kathleen Somers's spirit had been shattered by the loss of her husband and the transformation of her once-loving son, and she turned away from God. But Dr. Jared Matthews offered hope. Could the doctor heal her heart and help her regain her faith, in God and in love?

Don't miss

WHAT THE HEART KNOWS
On sale January 2004

Available at your favorite retail outlet.